Is There Anyone There?

Tony Brennan

Is There Anyone There?

& other stories

Is There Anyone There? & other stories
ISBN 978 1 76041 179 4
Copyright © text Tony Brennan 2016
Cover photo: man in shadow © Lasha Kilasonia

First published 2016 by
GINNINDERRA PRESS
PO Box 3461 Port Adelaide 5015
www.ginninderrapress.com.au

Contents

The Soy Sauce Valkyrie

Mr Will Wright decided something in his life simply had to change: he could no longer go on like this; it wasn't right. Will made that life-changing decision facing himself in the mirror shaving, at exactly ten minutes past six o'clock in the morning of his forty-second birthday.

The day had started as it had for the last twenty-one years. Nothing had changed, so what on earth could be the matter with him? Perhaps he was having a mid-life crisis? He had heard of those. But what had caused this…this…this deadly feeling of nothingness? He picked up the razor again, and then paused…why was he bothering to shave? But, his conscience rebuked him, he'd be late for work if he didn't get a move on. Will still hesitated… What if he *were* late? What if he never went back to that boring, mind-destroying job ever again? What if he just ran away? Oh, no, once again his conscience smote him, he couldn't do that…could he? Because if he did, what about his wife? Oh dear…that's right, the wife! Will forced himself to consider the woman he had married. Did she even care for him at all now? Or, worse still, did he really care for her?

He remembered, as if it were yesterday, how ecstatic with love he had been for the woman in the beginning. Perhaps it was the name that was starting to pall. Well, you don't find too many Brunhildas around, that's for sure; it was not the usual sort of name you would give to a child. Ah, but then, Brunhilda was no ordinary woman, was she? And she certainly didn't come from an ordinary background. Far from it!

Will thought of the Chinese Valkyries café where he first met his wife. The Valkyries was definitely unusual – for a Chinese café, that is. First of all, take the owner, his wife's father, Mr Siegfried Wong. He was a surprise and no mistake: a frustrated musician with a passion for Wagner who, forced to take over the family business, did so on his own terms. He had decorated the entire premises in the manner of *Neuschwanstein* – even the salt cellars were in the shape of swans – while Wagnerian music was pumped out of the sound system every moment the restaurant was open. Mr Wong mainly favoured the Ring Cycle; that was used most of the time.

Naturally enough, the shop had prospered, especially with opera buffs, and the New Nazis movement, but the strangest thing was that Mr Wong's beautiful daughter, whom he had named appropriately, Brunhilda, didn't like Wagner's music at all. She was into country and western, and hated the Ring Cycle. To express her rebellion, she did her long black hair in a country and western singer's style, wore a cowboy hat and boots with high heels. However, being enchantingly pretty, she was able to get away with it – in spite of her father's disapproval.

It was strange how Brunhilda and Will had taken to each other so quickly. Will was a very straight guy with a real dread of anything unusual, whereas Brunhilda was the opposite. It was she who did the running. Just as well, of course. Will would never have got around to it; he was desperately shy with women. Brunhilda began slipping him the extra curried prawn, the extra dim sim, or even the extra swan-cup of soy sauce, and very soon, even he, slow as he was, got the message that this beautiful girl was keen on him.

Brunhilda soon had them officially engaged, and it was she who planned the entire wedding, and what a wedding it was going to be! It was one that would exhibit her unique character to perfection. It also left Will with very painful memories – together with a permanent limp, which still troubled him when the wind was in the east.

Brunhilda decided that the ceremony would be something different: nothing boring or old-fashioned about it, and definitely no opera music at all. Will Wright was so stunned by the speed by which everything was happening, that he agreed to everything without really thinking much about it. However, he did begin to worry when he heard that Brunhilda insisted on having the wedding conducted – with everyone, guests included – wearing roller skates; he had never skated in his life. His loving fiancée arranged lessons for him, but he was never very good at it. He apologised many times to her, but she was sweet about it, and kept telling him it was OK – it would be super on the day.

It was to be a street wedding: al fresco, Brunhilda called it. The roller skating would make it perfect. People would talk about it for years afterwards.

Unfortunately, that certainly was true; people did talk about it, but for all the wrong reasons. On the day, everyone actually had turned up wearing roller skates, and the valiant minister managed to remain upright, but it was just after they had signed the register that disaster struck.

Will discovered – at that very moment – that his wife, Brunhilda Wong, was going to keep her own name, and not take his! This was such a shock to Will, that – while trying to juggle the names in his head: 'Mr Wright and Mrs Wong' – he moved jerkily in his agitation, forgetting he was on skates. He had also forgotten that they were standing on the side of a hill! Poor Will went charging off down the street gathering more and more speed as he went, only to crash into a policeman directing traffic at the main intersection.

The policeman went flying; the fifteen cars waiting for the signal saw the policeman's arm come down, and tore through the intersection into twenty-two other cars and trucks. The wedding guests rushed to aid the injured – forgetting that they, too, were wearing roller skates! Talk about bedlam! Will Wright ended up with a broken leg. The other accidents were much more dramatic – and had more serious outcomes.

However, every ill wind brings some good: the caterers did well out of it. There were no guests left to eat the food, so the waiters sat down and had a grand old feast, while the wedding guests were being treated by ambulance crews or at the emergency wards at the city hospitals. Brunhilda's father was seen hobbling on crutches and uttered many swear words to the medics, but as he said them in Mandarin, he didn't upset anyone.

At the hospital, in Emergency, Will was in terrible pain. Brunhilda, completely unharmed by the fiasco, told the triage nurse she was Mrs

Wong, so Will, naturally, was booked in as Mr Wong. He tried to correct this by saying he was not Wong, but Wright, but that nurse, and all the medical staff, thought he was agreeing by saying 'right'.

Before the operation to set his leg, he was in considerable discomfort, and the doctor asked breezily, 'Everything all right, Mr Wong?'

'Wright,' he corrected.

'Good, if you don't need the morphine, all the better for you, Mr Wong.' The doctor moved away.

'Wright,' Will moaned feebly.

Coming out of the anaesthetic was terrible. Every time they asked him a question, they said 'Mr Wong' and he automatically corrected them by saying 'Wright', so he got no alleviation of his pain. He thought that Brunhilda would soon fix up the error. However, he was surprised to hear she was out shopping for new swimwear. She said it was ridiculous not to use at least one of the tickets they had paid for, so off she went off to Bali, on her own, for the honeymoon.

It was not much of a honeymoon for Will. He had read, of course, about honeymoons in the magazines he found at the barber shop, but it did come as a surprise to know that he would spend his honeymoon in hospital, on his own, with his leg in traction. It didn't seem right, somehow.

Once out of hospital and back to work again, Will Wright was called into his superior officer, who demanded to know why he had changed his name to Wong. Didn't he realise that it was against company policy without permission? Will tried to explain, but the boss found it very suspicious; there were muttered whisperings going on in corners of the office. It was a very unpleasant time.

Gradually, however, the questions eased, and Will resumed his ordinary schedule, working hard to provide all the luxuries that Brunhilda demanded. The future stretched before him: dim, depressing and endlessly the same. There was a rebellion stirring within this quiet man; he felt defeated and, in a strange way, cheated. He often wondered whether if children had come it might have been different, but as it was, as the years rolled on, he found he was tired of his wife, and she seemed truly tired of him as well. Will often dreamed of running away to a tropical island somewhere, and just giving up everything, including his wife with her silly nonsense about the names.

Will had no one to confide in; all his neighbours thought he had changed his name and dutifully called him Mr Wong. He tried to correct this mistake in the beginning, only to be told, again and again, 'But your wife is Mrs Wong'; it was pointless, so he gave up. He often wondered just who he actually was: Mr Wright or Mr Wong.

But a chance occurrence changed his whole life – and, eventually, that of his wife. Will hardly ever gambled. Perhaps once a year, he might spend a dollar in a sweep at work, but that was that. Two weeks before his birthday, feeling disoriented and distinctly weary of life, he happened to be passing a newsagent, and going in bought a lottery ticket. A mischievous imp whispered in his ear while he was filling out the details, and as a result – almost without knowing it – Will used a new name which he had just invented: Mr Wrong. Well, the imp told him, without mincing words, it fitted, didn't it? He had done everything wrong so far. Having made this one and only feeble stand against a flint-faced fate, Will promptly forgot all about it, and never bothered to look up the results.

He wouldn't have known about the ticket had he not returned to that particular shop to buy a newspaper, on his way to work on his birthday, and the girl remembered him because of the strange name.

'Oh, Mr Wrong, I'm so glad you came back. We didn't know what to do about your ticket.'

'Ticket?' Will honestly didn't know what she was talking about and, he wondered, who was Mr Wrong?

'Yes, your lottery ticket,' the young lady smiled kindly at this middle-aged man. 'We have the pleasure to tell you that you've won second prize.' She pulled a little playful grimace. 'It wasn't the top prize. However, it's still pretty wonderful. What on earth will you do with two million dollars? Oh!' The attendant had to rush around to the other side of the counter; the customer appeared to be about to faint. 'Mr Wrong, Mr Wrong, are you all right?'

'Wright.'

'No, you're not right. You just sit here and I'll get you a glass of water. It's been a shock, I can see that.' The kind girl sat Will down and admonished him, as she moved away, 'Now, don't move, Mr Wrong, I'll be back in a jiffy.'

'Wright,' he muttered weakly.

'Yes, that's right.' The girl dashed off and returned with the water.

As Will sipped the liquid, he slowly began to realise that he had actually won two million dollars, and it was in the name of Wrong. He remembered his fit of pique which made him use that name. Two million dollars! Was that right? Who actually owned it? Mr Wright, Mr Wong, or Mr Wrong? In his mind, he saw a door of escape beginning to open.

When he felt that he could speak coherently, he asked the girl what he had to do, and it turned out to be very simple. She had to sign a document that she, personally, had sold him the ticket, and he could collect the money. She told him that if he filled in the form now and she signed it, they could fix it all up electronically if he wrote down his bank details. Will did as she told him at once, and he left the shop walking, if not on air, certainly on the right side of the path, and he felt at least fifteen years younger: life might be salvaged after all! Mr Wrong had become Mr Right, in his mind, and he, then and there, made a new resolution: he would remain Mr Wrong permanently. He also realised that, at last, he had a way out of his situation with Brunhilda. He could now just disappear, and no one, not even Brunhilda, would know where he was.

Will didn't go on to work that day, nor did he return to his home. When his boss rang his home to find out why he wasn't at work, his wife couldn't help him. He asked her what her name was, and she insisted she was Mrs Wong. So, Will's boss decided, that no-good Will did change his name after all. All his protestations had been lies; he'd thought as much at the time.

Mrs Wong realised the next day, when the morning tea was not on the bedside table when she awoke, that her husband was not there. She rang all her friends to ask their advice, and they hastened to her with serious faces, carrying fattening pastries, and asked her if she had phoned the police.

'Police?' she queried, alarmed.

'Yes, Mrs Wong, in case there has been an accident. Your poor husband could be lying unconscious in a hospital somewhere. You must notify the police.'

'Goodness! I never thought of that.'

With her neighbours watching and eating greedily, in order, as they said, to keep their strength up, Mrs Wong phoned the police. They took down the particulars and started a check on all hospitals, and other obvious places, but the search was negative. No one had any knowledge of a Mr Will Wong.

Feeling desperately unhappy, Mrs Wong hauled herself out of bed and, dressing quickly, went to see her father. Mr Wong senior – his left eye still covered with an eyepatch – made it clear to his daughter that it was entirely her fault her husband had left her, and if she wanted to come back to work for him, she would have to obey new rules: lose weight and dress appropriately for his restaurant – his patrons would not tolerate her in her former cowboy outfit. She meekly agreed, went on a ghastly diet, and dressed as ordered.

Three long, sad years passed, with Brunhilda now a pretty, slim, middle-aged woman, but still longing for her husband. She was now earning very good money, not only at the shop, but as an expert in Wagnerian music, having decided that, if you couldn't beat it, you might as well try to profit by it. She entered one competition after another, and eventually won International Mastermind – her category, Wagner's Ring Cycle – and was acclaimed as one of the few persons in the whole world who knew the entire score of the Cycle by heart and could recite all the words from memory. The City Opera Company even gave her a presentation gift of a complete Valkyrie outfit – which she wore in the shop – in gratitude for the publicity she had given them. Brunhilda rather liked the outfit; it suited her, though the long horns were a little awkward at times, especially if they were using lanterns strung across the restaurant for festive occasions – they tended to get tangled; as did that poor man's toupee, which she unintentionally snagged. It was made worse because Brunhilda, being totally unaware of the disaster, carried on serving with the piece swinging crazily on the tip of one horn. The customer had turned a bright red chasing after the waitress to retrieve it. However, with her new celebrity status and her spectacular outfit, the profits of the shop soared, and her photo was in all the papers.

Will Wrong, idling in his hammock at a tropical island resort, with one bare foot lazily tapping to the music of the band on the beach, saw the picture of his one-time wife in the papers, and marvelled both at her appearance and her new fame. He was suddenly smitten with remorse at the way he had treated his wife. His old love for the pretty girl he had married flared into existence again, and he wanted her to be with him. He knew his happiness would then be complete. He glanced at the date on the top of the page, and decided it was exactly the right day to contact her. It was on the anniversary of their marriage.

Will began to worry if, after all that had happened, his wife might not want to come back to him. He came up with a plan. She was now a quiz champion, so if she bothered to answer his quiz he would know she does still care for him. Lying back in his hammock, Will picked up his phone.

In the Chinese café, Brunhilda's mobile rang; she picked it up and said automatically, 'Valkyries Chinese Restaurant.' She was startled to hear a man's voice chuckling, followed by a burst of the Valkyries' war cry sung in a loud male voice. 'Who is it?' she asked tremblingly, hoping desperately it was her roving Will.

'It's your prince, otherwise known as Mr Right, but also known as Will.'

'Where are you?'

'You'll have to work that out. You're now famous at quizzes so listen carefully. First clue, four letters: if you have one of these in your saddle, the horse will buck.'

'Say that again.' Brunehila thought for a moment, and said, 'Burr.'

'That's right. Second clue, pay attention now: a state of mind involving the emotions when something good, or bad, has happened. Four letters.'

'Gracious me,' Brunhilda's mind was rapidly surveying the possibilities. 'Right, I've got it. It's mood.'

'Good! Third clue: an exclamation.'

'That's all, Mr Wright?'

'Wrong. It's Wrong now.'

'But I haven't given you the answer yet, so how can you say…'

'Tell me the answer,' Will interrupted.

Brunhilda replied, 'The last syllable is "ah". The whole word is Ber-mud-a.'

Will congratulated her. 'You're right.'

'Yes, I know, Mr Wright.'

'Not Wright, but Wrong.'

'But you told me it was right.'

There was a slight pause.

Will took a deep breath and continued. 'Now listen, Brunhilda, I love my wife, and miss my princess greatly. I'm sorry I ran off. Could you possibly forgive me and come and join me? We'll have such fun on this island? You would? Oh, that makes me so happy. But a word of warning, dearest, don't ask for Wright.'

'So it's Wong?'

'No, it not Wong. It's Wrong.'

'Well, I can't ask for anyone until I know who it is.'

'I told you, it's Wrong. Listen, Brunhilda, just come here to the Castaway Calypso Club, and don't ask for Wright or Wong, just Wrong. Got it?'

'No.'

'Well, get it.'

'Got it.'

'Right.'

'But you said it was Wrong.'

'Listen, it was Wright, but became Wong, but it's now Wrong, right?'

'It's Wrong-Wright, is that it?'

'Just Wrong, just Wrong, Wrong, Wrong, Wrong. Got it?'

'Right!'

'That's right.'

Brunhilda put down the phone understandably puzzled; it sounded suspiciously wrong to her, but the truth of the matter was, that's how Wright and Wong became Wrong, which, of course, turned out to be right.

The High Life

'Madam, are you sure you have the right hotel?' the commissionaire asked as he opened the door of the cab. He stared down at the woman struggling to get out.

She was wearing a magnificent mink coat, but on her head was a large colourful beanie, with a thick, nodding, pompom with Mickey Mouse on the top; her shoes were scuffed and worn down at the heels, and her thick woollen stockings had darns clearly visible.

With an effort, Dolly Dobbs struggled out of the cab clutching a large brown paper package. 'It is the Majestic Grand, isn't it, duckie?'

'Yes, but…'

'Just as well! Thought we must have come to the wrong place! I told the driver it was the Majestic we wanted. I knew he wouldn't take us to the wrong place. Nice chap, got corns you know. Gave him an old remedy, handed down from my old Mum it was, and he was ever so grateful, didn't want to take a tip. But I said to Dicky, "No, we must do the right thing now we've started," and Dicky agreed – we gave him fifty cents!'

The taxi driver was busy hauling out the fourteen pieces of luggage – old suitcases, parcels in brown paper, and some clothes bundled into plastic bags. He looked at the doorman, rolled his eyes, pulled a face, jumped into the driving seat, and took off at a great speed.

'A whole fifty cents! Goodness, that must have changed his day, madam. But seriously, madam, are you actually staying at this hotel?'

This caused a burst of merry laughter from the tall, elderly lady. 'Well, we didn't come all this way from London to sleep on the footpath, lad. Of course we are! For the entire winter. Going skiing we are, Dicky and me. Oh, dear!' Dolly leant over her suitcases and pointed to a tiny stain on the doorman's uniform coat. 'You've spilt something on your pretty jacket.

Look, dearie, never mind – no one will notice it. When we've unpacked – up in the penthouse – pop the jacket up to me and I'll soon have that stain out in a jiffy. No one need ever know.'

'The penthouse, madam?' the doorman asked weakly, his eyes searching for the stain.

'Well, we wanted the best, you see. We've never done this before.' Dolly nudged the doorman in the ribs. 'To tell the truth, we've never had the lolly before.' She let loose a peal of loud laughter. 'But now, the sky's the limit, so come along, help Dicky with the luggage and let's get inside. It's freezing out here.'

'It usually is, madam, in a ski resort.'

'Now you're laughing at me,' Dolly chided. 'Let's get inside and see the manager and find our suite. Oh, doesn't that sound grand? Our suite.'

With both Mr and Mrs Dobbs helping, all the bits and pieces of luggage were taken into the foyer. While Dolly was gasping at the beauty of the enormous foyer, a thin, beautifully dressed man of forty came forward to meet them.

'Mr and Mrs Dobbs? From England?'

The elderly couple nodded.

'I am Mr Fortescue, the manager. We received your telegram – in fact all of your telegrams.' He spoke in a cultivated, superior British voice.

'That's right, love! We wanted to make sure that the booking was secure. Ooer! What a beautiful place you've got here – fair takes my breath away – it's gigantic! Oh, it must be lovely to work in such a glorious place! How many cleaners do you have?'

'I beg your pardon, madam?'

'Oh hundreds, I suppose,' Dolly went on, not heeding the manager. 'You'd need 'em for something this big.' Dolly turned to her husband. 'Well, Dicky, let's get up to our room – I'm tired, it's been a long journey.'

'If you would just sign in here, sir. The desk manager manoeuvred his way around the pile of luggage to the desk.

Dicky Dobbs rubbed his jet-lagged eyes, put on his glasses and signed the register.

'Forgive me checking, sir,' the suavely courteous Mr Fortescue asked, 'but you are staying for the whole of the winter?'

'You're bloomin' right we are,' replied Dicky, 'and we're going to buy a whole lot of flash new clothes and gear, and we're going to learn to ski while we're here.'

'I'm sure, sir, that you'll be very happy here. In the arcade, leading from the foyer, are all the very best shops, and you do not need to worry about paying for each item as you shop. All the stores are owned by the hotel, so they will automatically transfer the amount to your central account here. You can finalise the account when you actually are about to leave. We have beauty parlours…'

'I don't think I'll be using the beauty parlours, son, but the missus now – well, you never know.' Dicky leaned over confidentially to the manager. 'I don't really know just what Dolly's got in mind. You see,' Dicky whispered, 'we've never had money before, but now! Who knows what we'll do? I mean, twelve million pounds is a lot…'

'Twelve million, sir?' gasped the manager faintly.

'Give or take some. I'm not good at sums, and your dollars confuse me – I don't know what that amount is in dollars. Dolly does all the finance stuff.' Dicky turned to his wife. 'Are you ready, love? Well, pack up now and off we go – we'll need a couple of trips, I think.'

'No, no, no, sir, I beg of you…stop,' the manager rushed to the elderly couple. He looked angrily around for porters, and saw two hurrying towards him. 'Don't touch anything, I beg of you. The porters here will carry all your things up to your suite.' He spoke sharply to the porters: 'The penthouse suite.'

Dolly looked surprised but refused to surrender the large parcel she was carrying. Mr Fortescue bowed and led the two new guests over to the luxurious lifts, which whisked them silently and speedily up to the top floor. He overrode their protests, and persisted in coming with them.

Arriving at their penthouse stop, they stepped from the lift straight into their beautiful hall. Going through the hall, Dolly and Dicky were surprised to see four maids standing to attention by the entrance to the lounge.

Dolly's keen eyes swept over the huge room and she exclaimed in dismay. 'Oh, no! That's terrible!'

The manager was frantic. What on earth could be wrong? The suite was magnificent; only the richest people on earth were ever able to stay in it.

He found his voice. 'My dear Mrs Dobbs, whatever is the matter?'

'Oh, it's so big! Oh dear! I've so looked forward to this holiday – the first one in all our married life, and when I look at this…!'

'But what is wrong with it? We can change anything you would like altered.'

'No, I wouldn't change anything! It's beautiful, just like you had in that glossy magazine I read at the fish shop – they'd used it to wrap the chips. That's where I got the idea of coming to this place. No, the place is wonderful but, it's…it's…the cleaning.'

'The cleaning?'

'Yes, I didn't think I'd be spending all my time on holiday cleaning, and the size of this place…'

The Fortescue, the manager, signalled to the four maids to disappear and said quietly, 'Mr and Mrs Dobbs, I think we'd better have a little talk, don't you? Let's go into the snuggery – it's like a little breakfast room – and while I get one of the maids to make a cup of tea for you, I think I'll explain how things are done in a big hotel. Agreed?'

'Agreed,' both Dolly and Dicky said fervently, while Dolly added, 'And if you want any mending done, Mr Fortescue, while I'm here, just let me know. You're being so very kind to us.'

'Mending? God in Heaven!' He looked angrily around. 'Where's that blasted tea?'

Dolly unwrapped her parcel and she held up a large kitchen teapot. 'I've got the pot, Mr Fortescue, and Dicky could easily find a few tea bags in one of the parcels. Oh, I'm so hungry. Do you think Dicky could slip out and buy a couple of buns or something to have with our tea? I don't know what time you eat at the hotel.'

The manager wondered if he could survive much more. He led

the couple to the small kitchen area of the suite, took the teapot from Dolly, gave it to a maid, who had miraculously appeared, and raised his eyebrows. She nodded and disappeared while he picked up the phone, and said, brusquely, 'Room service.'

Within five minutes, Dolly and Dicky were astonished to be sitting at a feast which was being served to them by a waiter – there were English crumpets, hot and dripping with butter, small delicious sandwiches, tiny mouth-watering cakes, and even scones. Dolly had removed her beautiful mink coat and sat revealed in a garish, shocking-pink pants-suit of a fleecy material. She removed the beanie from her head and her long, thick, grey hair fell down. Dicky had removed his shoes and his coat and sat at the table with his braces showing, and his toes in the darned socks exploring the depth of the beautiful carpet.

Mr Fortescue had explained the miracle of twenty-four-hour room service – they could actually order anything they wanted to eat at any time day or night! But, when he saw the couple revealed in all their shabby and cheap attire, he took a brave decision. 'Mr Dobbs, and Mrs Dobbs, may I speak freely and personally to you? You are going to be with us for nearly three months, and I want you to have the most wonderful holiday of your life...'

'That's downright nice of you, lad,' declared Dicky. 'Ever since we arrived in your wonderful country, people have been so nice to us. Americans are very friendly people. More so than back home, I think – well, to people like us, I mean.'

'He's right, Mr Fortescue,' chimed in Dolly. 'Do you know, when we first decided to use our inheritance, and see a bit of the life we see on the movies, people back home were so snobby. If it hadn't been for Aggie – that's the Duchess of Monmouth, she made us call her Aggie – her real name is Agatha. Well, she was the only one who made a friend of us. We've stayed at her castle, and she made us sit with her at the high table. But I've interrupted you again, Mr Fortescue. What were you going to say?'

'Would you please forgive me for saying that you need different clothes, and perhaps some personal attention to your appearance, to help you fit in more easily here at the hotel – I just don't want you to be insulted by other guests.'

'Oh dear,' Dolly answered. 'I know we've got all the wrong things and don't know how to dress, or anything really. Would you really do that for us, Mr Fortescue? I mean, we're nobodies.'

The manager beamed. 'Just leave it to me.' He picked up the phone again, 'Get me Madame Blandois, Madame Corinne and Monsieur Henri and tell them to come to the penthouse immediately.'

For the next four hours, Dolly and Dicky felt as though they had been accidentally involved in a whirlwind of fantasy. They had been inspected by a superior-looking woman with a French accent, who actually did come from France, and spent most of her time tut-tutting over Dolly's clothes; then a Madame Corinne with a phoney French accent – who had never travelled outside America – took over. She took hold of Dolly's hair, and examined her face as if it were a blank canvas, while the French gentleman, called Henri, made poor Dicky walk around before him stripped to his undies and measured him, and then both guests were hauled off to the exquisite salons on the ground floor. Before leaving, they had given permission for the maids to unpack their clothes and left it to them to decide which ones to throw away.

When Dolly and Dicky came back, they found their wardrobes empty – everything had been thrown out, and lists were made of what had to be replaced.

Mr Fortescue had been as good as his word. While Dolly and Dicky were recovering from the shock of what had been done to them downstairs, and peering continually into the mirror to try to see if they looked the slightest bit like they did when they had arrived at the hotel, one of the maids – her name was Juanita – announced they had a guest. It turned out to be Hans, a very good-looking tanned young man with a Swiss accent, who informed them that he would be their ski instructor. Their first lesson would be the next morning. He also told them that their new ski clothes would be delivered to them by the evening, along with all the other clothes they would need. He had been instructed by the manager to tell them that.

That evening, they dressed in their new clothes and stood side by side looking into the full-length mirror.

'Blimey, love,' Dicky declared, 'I feel frightened. You look like a duchess that I don't know, and I need an introduction to myself. Who are we, for heaven's sake!'

'Now, Dicky,' Dolly admonished, 'we are a fabulously wealthy, elderly couple, that's who we are. I think you look very handsome and distinguished – a little like an American senator.'

'And you my dear,' responded Dicky, 'look absolutely stunning. That dress is magnificent, the jewellery is simply breath-taking, and your hair and make-up is simply amazing. You look…beautiful, love.'

'Well, now's the test, Dicky. We've got to enter the main restaurant downstairs. Mr Fortescue promised he would help us with all the problems – you know, with cutlery, the names of the dishes, and the wines…'

'It's the wines I'm worried about,' admitted Dicky. 'I don't know anything about wine, and they'll ask me. I don't suppose I can say the only one I know is a rough red.'

'We'll manage, dear. Mr Fortescue won't let us down and then we begin to learn to ski tomorrow morning.' She clapped her hands in her excitement. 'Pinch me, dear. I think I'm dreaming.' Dolly let out a little scream. 'Oh, Dicky! I didn't mean it literally! Come on, let's go.'

In actual fact, the dinner was a breeze. The manager had wised up the waiters assigned to their table, and had arranged to have Madame Corinne with her beautiful, phoney French accent, and her exquisite clothes, sit at their table to teach them – by letting them see her choose the right cutlery and glassware first.

The following six weeks sped by in a happy and exciting series of days. Within a couple of weeks, Dolly and Dicky were totally at home in their new sphere. They were fit and strong, in spite of their sixty-plus years, and learned to ski very easily. They skied every morning on the easier slopes, then had a long luxurious soak in the warm-water spa followed by a delicious, long morning tea, at which they insisted the four maids joined them. They had come to know the maids well: Juanita, Rosa, Maria, and Magdala – their lives, their families, their boyfriends and their problems – and the maids loved them. They prayed that these strange, eccentric British people would stay forever.

Dolly and Dicky had come to know Madame Corinne well also, and discovered that she was in love with Ted Fortescue but was desperate, as he was so slow that Corinne was becoming frantic.

'I'm thirty-seven,' she confided to Dolly and Dicky at the table one night. 'If he doesn't say something soon, I'll have to leave and try working somewhere else. I might meet someone who will be interested in me then – it's the only hope I have left.'

A few days after this confidence, Dolly was talking to Ted Fortescue, now her friend. 'I'm thinking, Ted, of taking Corinne back with me to England. She's been a godsend to us at the dinner table;. We're able to function perfectly now, and it's all because of her. I need her – she could be my personal companion, and I could then introduce her to a number of eligible men, for she's a very beautiful girl…'

There was a strangled sort of sound from the manager. 'Take her away?'

'Yes, she's wasting her time here. She's cut out to be a wife and mother. I know a baronet back in England. Not much to look at – weak chin, no conversation, not many brains – but his mother's desperate for him to have an heir, as the line ends with him. I know he'd be interested, and Corinne would have a title as well as a family. Um, yes, the more I think of it, the more I like the idea. Oh well, off to the shops… I do so love your wonderful shops here in the hotel, Ted.'

And, indeed she did. There were dozens of new dresses, shoes, underclothes, not to mention a mountain of jewellery which she wore with dignified elegance. They would need really good suitcases when they left, so they bought them in the hotel shop. Dolly was so glad that Corinne had left her hair grey – as had Henri with Dicky. However, whatever they had done to both their heads, the grey was now silver and looked magnificent. With her long expensive evening dinner gowns, and her beautiful coiffed hair, she looked every inch an aristocrat. Both Dolly's and Dicky's speech had altered. They were both good mimics, and were soon speaking English, not in their original cockney version, but as the Americans believed royalty spoke in Britain. Visitors to the hotel asked their friends who were the elegant aristocratic British couple.

The legend of the nobility was heightened by an incident one day in the foyer after dinner. A very rich old American lady, laden with diamonds, was attempting to discover just who these Dobbses really were. She thought there was something fishy about them. Dolly parried the questions well, but was glad of an interruption from the maid, Juanita. Dolly had asked Juanita to find details of an upcoming event at the hotel. Juanita, finding the information Dolly required, set out to let this eccentric but wonderful wealthy lady know. She stood just outside the group which was talking in the foyer, until Dolly happened to see her.

She turned to Juanita, who, shy girl that she was, blushed, curtseyed slightly and said, 'I'm sorry, my lady...'

She got no further. Dolly, with great presence of mind, covered Juanita's hand with her own and said in an audible whisper, 'No, dear, just Mrs Dobbs please...remember what I told you?'

Mrs van Stuger was triumphant! At last she knew the truth. Dolly Dobbs was travelling incognito; she was a lady of the aristocracy. When she tackled Dolly with this, Dolly smiled gently and, excusing herself, retired to her suite.

Dolly was not surprised to find Corinne waiting for her. Dolly took her in her arms and congratulated her. Corinne was surprised; how did she know? Dolly laughed and asked when the wedding would be, because if she was still there, she and her husband would like to attend.

At the end of six weeks, the idyll came to a difficult patch. Dolly had gone for a walk down the pretty little resort town; and the switchboard receptionist received a phone call that startled her. It was from Wales in Britain. Mr Fortescue was at the desk and the receptionist beckoned to him. She turned the speaker on and both heard the clipped precise English voice.

'I am phoning for Her Grace, Agatha, Duchess of Mommumble, mumble, mumble.'

The receptionist apologised, fiddled with some knobs and managed to pick up the call again.

The voice was continuing, 'This is her secretary speaking. Her Grace wishes to speak to Mrs Dorothy Dobbs, or her husband, Richard Dobbs. Would you please connect me to their suite?'

The telephonist was excited: a real duchess! 'Please hold the line madam, I'm connecting you now.'

'Mrs Dobbs? Oh, forgive me, it's Mr Dobbs! Is Mrs Dobbs at home? Her Grace wishes to speak to her. No? Well, would you please take the call? Thank you.'

The secretary's voice was replaced by the beautiful cultured voice of the duchess.

'Dicky-bird, is that you? Where is that naughty wife of yours? Oh, I see, painting the town red's more like it. Listen Dicky, something frightful happened. My poor old Cecil conked out at last... Well, it was a bit shattering, poor old thing...had to have three gins to get over it... Yes, I do miss him. Got used to him, I expect – I suppose you do a bit, after forty years. Had a retriever bitch years ago, was devastated when she died, had her for sixteen years. Feel the same way now... Well, I miss you both too. The two of you are really the only true friends I have... No, I'm dreading the year of mourning – I'll have to stay in this ghastly cold castle for a whole year draped in black, but I'll have to go through with it, for appearance's sake... What? Come over to join you in America. I've never been to America – they hate us, don't they? Something about tea, or something, can't remember. No? Well, what about the red Indians? I've seen those movies on the telly and it doesn't look very pleasant. You're sure? Beautiful? Is it really? And the hotel? The finest in the land and the staff are simply the greatest! Oh, Dicky, you're very naughty. I'm tempted, but I'd never be able to make the trip on my own – no, it's out of the question at my age. I suppose I could come, if you and Dolly were to come and get me, but I know that's out of the question. It isn't? But your time is just about up, isn't it? If I come, you would stay for a further month and see the place in the spring? You would come all the way here, and then fly back with me? Oh, dear, Dicky-bird, that's the kindest thing anyone has ever done for me… Well, I'm crying, actually, Dicky. Nobody has ever done that much for me in my whole life. I'm going to hang up, dear. I'm sorry to be such a soppy wimp, but tell Dolly I love her and I'll count the days until I see you both back here. If it all turns out, and Dolly approves, we'll paint the town red together! What a lark! Toodle-oo, pet.'

Two hours later, a very troubled Dolly came to Mr Fortescue's office. He immediately brought her in, and sat her in the most comfortable chair.

Dolly burst into speech. 'Oh, Ted, sometimes my husband gets carried away! I really don't know what to do!'

'Could you please explain to me, Mrs Dobbs, what the problem is,' enquired the manager gently. 'Perhaps I could help.'

'While I was out walking, Dicky took a call from Aggie – you know, the Duchess of Monmouth – and foolishly told her we'd go across to Wales, collect her and bring her back here for a good holiday.'

'I see.' Mr Fortescue kept his expression surprised – as though he had not heard the entire phone call. 'And what is the problem?'

'Well, I don't know whether you have any rooms left. And silly Dicky told Aggie that we'd stay on another month as well. Dear, oh dear, what a mess! We've only booked for one more month and then must leave, don't we?'

'Let me see the register, Mrs Dobbs. I think we could arrange for another month and I don't see any problem in catering for the duchess – we could easily fit her in one of the other great suites.'

'Oh, you are such a comfort, Ted. So it needn't be a disaster after all? You see,' she added confidentially, 'I don't want to offend Aggie in any way. She was the one who came to our rescue socially in England – we owe her such a lot.'

'Yes, I do understand, dear Mrs Dobbs. How long would you be away?'

'What do you think? I thought about two days to get back to Wales, stay three days to get over the flight, and then two days to get back – we'd be away for a week. Would that be all right?'

'Perfectly. Now what about your jewellery in the safe? You'd want to take some of that to wear back home, wouldn't you?' Ted Fortescue smiled roguishly. 'That'll be a shock to those you insulted you. And make sure you take some of those beautiful new clothes as well.'

Dolly's eyes filled with tears. She took the manager's hand and held it firmly. 'You have made our time here the most wonderful time of our lives, Ted. No, I'm going upstairs, otherwise I'll start bawling my eyes out. Just give me the jewel case and I'll have a look – up in the suite – and bring it back when I've chosen a few bits and pieces. I'll leave nearly all of it here with you in the safe.'

The manager was absent for only a couple of minutes and handed Dolly her beautiful jewel case, which was the size of a small suitcase. Dolly took the case, leant forward and kissed the startled man on the cheek, and rushed out.

The next day was a hive of activity. Dicky got reservations on the plane, using their return tickets. Dolly and the maids packed frantically, leaving half of all the beautiful clothes in the wardrobes; even so, by the time they had finished, they had two of the best new very large suitcases filled, packed to the brim, plus much hand luggage.

The next morning, Dolly and Dicky dressed with great care and Dolly wore her beautiful mink coat – she called it her lucky coat – and then came the farewells to the maids, to Corinne, and to all the friends they had made, including Hans the ski instructor. Dolly kept reminding them all that they would only be away for a week, but even if anything unforeseen kept them longer, it would only be a few days more than that. A crowd of their friends – waiters, maids and guests – came to the steps of the hotel to see them off.

The porters carried out the suitcases and hand luggage to the taxi. Dolly and Dicky saw, to their delight, that it was the original driver who had brought them to the hotel.

He was beaming. 'No fare this time, honey! Your cure worked

wonders. Never felt so good for years – run a mile every morning now. Now hop in. I'll fix the luggage.'

As the taxi drove away from the hotel, Dolly had genuine tears in her eyes as she waved goodbye. Dicky held her hand tightly. He managed to keep the conversation going with the driver, but it was not until they were in the international airport at JFK that they were able to relax completely and speak without reservation.

'Ready to go back, dear?'

'Certainly am, love. We've done pretty well so far.'

'It's the coat, I think. One look at that, and people immediately imagine I'm rolling in dough.'

'Little do they know,' laughed Dicky. 'Bought for five quid from that loony woman you cleaned for,' he chuckled.

'Silly woman,' his wife added. 'Suddenly became an animal liberationist and couldn't get rid of it quickly enough – before her friends saw she still had it.'

They both laughed heartily.

'Have we got enough with us? I brought all I could.' Dicky pulled up the sleeves of his coat and there were three real gold watches on his arm while several rings winked on his fingers. 'Every pocket is full as well,' he added. 'What about you?'

'Yes, I think so, love. Look!' Dolly pulled up the sleeves of her mink coat and the full, loose-fitting sleeves of her frock, revealing her arms covered with glittering diamond bracelets. Around her neck she wore not only a diamond necklace but her fabulous pearls as well. Her fingers were covered in exquisite rings.

Dicky looked admiringly at his wife. 'I meant to ask you, Dolly, what did you put in the jewel case that I took back to Fortescue? It was very heavy.'

'While I was out walking – and doing my duchess impersonation trick, Dicky – I picked up two half-bricks from a construction site,' she laughed. 'I think dear Ted will get a shock when they eventually open the jewel.'

Dicky smiled, then took his wife's arm and went to the desk. 'It's been very exciting, love, but it'll be good to be back home for a spell.'

'Well, Dicky,' responded Dolly, 'we didn't do too badly – and all for the price of a return economy air ticket!'

Laughing, they took their places in the queue at the airport desk.

*

Ten days later, Ricky and Polly Saunders were sitting comfortably in their tiny London terrace house eating muffins with their afternoon tea, while they were doing their sums.

'Well, Ricky,' Polly demanded. 'What final figure did you come up with? I've worked out what I think it should be roughly, and I've tried to make sure I've deducted all the expenses that I could remember. I was hoping for more dough for all the jewellery we didn't want, and the excess furs.'

'Still, love, we didn't do too badly,' Ricky answered. 'You know the miserly fences never give you a fraction of the real value – they're real crooks to my way of thinking. And as for that forger! To demand a thousand pounds for each passport in the new name was outrageous – talk about inflation! However, I think we've cleared a little over £47,792, Polly.' He smiled at his wife. 'Not bad for our very first venture, was it?'

'Not bad? It's bloomin' marvellous! Oh, I did so enjoy it – every minute of it. There were certainly dicey moments, but it was fun!' Polly responded happily. She carefully wiped her buttery fingers with a napkin and picked up a travel brochure. 'I've been thinking, Ricky. How do you feel about Venice for next winter? Or we could try Rome, and after that, there's Spain, and Russia and…'

Ricky nodded, happily. Being a senior citizen had never been such fun! 'We'll need another passport, love. This time I'd like a name with a bit of class behind it. What do you think of "de Vere", "Chalingworth-Beardsley" or "Forthswale-Smyth" or "Amberly-Honeysmith" or "Pottersby-Pimm"?'

'Hmmm?' Polly murmured. 'Then there's Australia, Japan, the exotic Middle East, Monte Carlo…'

Ricky smiled broadly and reached for another muffin.

The Negative Man

Simon Wilks was considered a very negative man. His son Trevor remarked, as he was leaving the house for work one morning, that it was a glorious day. Simon answered that it was, but it would rain before four o'clock in the afternoon. Trevor went off to work, muttering angrily under his breath about his father. The fact that it did rain before four o'clock in the afternoon only incensed Trevor the more.

In the evening, Sally, Simon's daughter, told her father she was going out to watch her boyfriend playing in an exhibition match, and she was certain he would be selected for the national team – everybody was certain of that.

'I'm sorry, dear, but he won't be,' objected her father. 'His playing is quite ordinary and he has a problem kicking. Until he can correct that, he'll be playing only in amateur games for the rest of his time.'

Sally was furious and went off in a huff and when Jonathan failed to please the selectors – for the very reasons mentioned by her father – she was even angrier with him.

Maud, Simon's wife, asked him to accompany her on Saturday morning to help her choose a dress for her niece's wedding. Simon was reluctant to do so but, in the interests of marital harmony, finally agreed to go with his wife.

In the expensive shop Maud had chosen, she tried on dress after dress, until she finally declared she had found the right one. 'Well, don't just sit there, Simon,' she demanded. 'I want an honest opinion: does this frock suit me or not?'

Simon looked closely at the frock and wondered what he could say. Maud was plump – in fact, she was more than plump, she was fat. The dress she had chosen was in brilliant reds and yellows, and was skin-tight over her stomach and her rear; neither of which could be called her most attractive attributes.

'Do you think, dear,' Simon hesitatingly said, 'that it's exactly right for you? I mean, it's absolutely lovely, no doubt about that, but perhaps it would be perfect for a less…er…exuberant figure?'

'What do you mean, exuberant? Are you saying I'm fat?'

'Perish the thought, Maud dear. I meant a generous figure, not exuberant.'

'And what does generous mean? Is that yet another way of saying I'm fat?'

'Well, all I can say, Maud, is that I think you'll be disappointed with that particular frock when you get home and your friends see it.'

'You're the very limit, Simon Wilks. I don't know how I've stayed with you all these years. You're never any help when I need your advice. All you can do is say horrible negative things all the time.'

'Which happen to be true,' muttered Simon bitterly, regretting that he had ever come out with Maud in the first place.

'What did you say?'

'I said I like you best in blue, Maud,' Simon lied.

That night when Maud was parading around the house in her new frock, her best friend, Fanny from next door, came in, took one look, and said, 'For the love of Mike! Did Simon make you buy that hideous dress? It's frightful. You can't go to the wedding wearing that. Everyone will laugh.'

Maud turned on Simon. 'You see, Simon, I was right. It's all your fault that I bought this frightful dress and wasted all that money.'

'Yes, dear,' Simon said resignedly. What was the use of saying anything else? He was always in the wrong.

After Fanny had gone, Maud, her daughter and her son called Simon into the kitchen.

Trevor took the chair – a kitchen chair actually. 'Now, Dad, something has to be done. We're all fed up to the teeth with your negative remarks about everything we do. We've decided that we want you to try your hardest to make a big change and go in the opposite direction. Would you give it a try?'

'I'm impressed with what you say, Trevor,' Simon answered sincerely. 'I'm sorry I've upset all of you; you know that's the last thing I ever want to do. I'll certainly try my hardest not to say another negative thing to anyone in this family.'

'Well, that's handsomely said, Dad,' conceded Trevor, and they shook hands like regular chaps.

Maud and Sally kissed Simon, and a new period in their lives began.

Trevor came to his father a few days later. 'Dad, you know I've paid for my unit, I'm doing well at work, and I've also saved a fair bit. I was reading a prospectus brochure the other day. It said if I invest in the Neverlie Minerals Company in Rangoon, I could get thirty-eight per cent return on my money. What do you think of that as an investment?'

Simon bit his lips and clasped his hand together under the table. He summonsed up a smile of admiration. 'Trevor, I knew you'd turn out to be a wonderful financial genius. It sounds…it sounds…it sounds a goldmine!'

Trevor was delighted and shook hands with his father. Within a week he had sold his unit, put all his saving in shares in the mineral company and discovered, to his horror, when all the money had gone, that the company didn't even exist, except on paper. He turned on his father. 'If you had only been less enthusiastic about that wretched, crooked company, I would never have ruined myself. It's all your fault.'

Simon sighed.

Sally was having doubts about her boyfriend, Jonathan, who Simon privately thought was a layabout – a sleazy lout without a brain in his head and one who would never do a day's work in his life. Sally came to her father and asked his advice on whether she should break off with Jonathan or not.

He was silent for a long while wondering just how he could answer. At last, gritting his teeth, he said, 'Sally, you know you're my favourite child. I want you to be as happy as the day is long. What do you think of Jonathan? I'm sure that what you think is right.'

'Oh, I'm so happy you said that, Dad,' Sally answered. 'I'll see him tonight and tell him we can be married straight away.' She kissed her father and danced out of the room.

Maud had another problem. 'Simon, I've got to decide on whether to take in a particular lodger or not. You said you'd leave the decision to me. We need the money now that poor Trevor was ill-advised about his investments and is ruined, so we have to take in a lodger, just to make ends meet, but I want to know what you really think.'

Simon had met the person in question and was convinced he was on the run from the police. He remembered his promise, however, and told Maud that she was always a wonderful judge of character and that he thought the chap was just the right one to have in the house.

Oh course, within a week, Jonathan, Sally's betrothed, had bolted with another girl who had a bit of money, and the lodger had been installed for only a few days when Maud noticed that the housekeeping money and all the good cutlery had gone, along with her grandmother's real silver teaspoons. The lodger had gone as well. Both mother and daughter blamed Simon immediately. Sally wept long and hard and told her father strongly that if it had not been for his endorsement, she would never have pledged herself to Jonathan, while Maud said that if Simon had not whole-heartedly approved of the dodgy lodger she would never have taken him in.

Simon sighed; he simply couldn't win.

Simon loved his family and truly wanted to please them, if it were ever possible to do so. He went to see a friend of his who had been a groundsman at the university so was considered the intellectual in the street. His name was Willy. Simon outlined his problem and told of all his attempts to do what his family wanted.

'Is there any other way, Willy?' he asked hopefully.

Willy paused, and stroked his chin thoughtfully – he had seen the professors do that as they walked in the gardens. Finally he spoke. 'Simon, there is another way.'

'There is? Oh, that's good news ,Willy. What must I do?'

'You must become a "maybe yes, maybe no" man.'

'I beg your pardon?'

'You know, indecisive, never give a real opinion at all. Then you can say when it turns out right, "I told you so" and when it doesn't, you can say, "I told you it wouldn't." You could vary the words a bit. For example, you could say, "Could be right, could be wrong" instead of "Maybe" – to give it a bit of variety.'

'I see,' Simon answered gratefully. 'Yes, I do understand. Thank you, Willy, you're a treasure and no mistake.'

For the next month, Simon put into practice exactly what Willy had recommended. At the end of the month, the family were ready to lynch him.

'What is the matter with you, Dad?' shouted Trevor. 'Can't you ever make up your mind?'

Sally actually screamed on one occasion, 'If you ever say maybe again, I think I'll leave home. It's driving me crackers.'

While Maud continued in the same vein for an interminable length – as was her wont.

Simon retired to the little back garden to think. He had to do something. He sat on an old upturned bucket for a full hour, and then the idea came to him. He hurried up stairs and quickly rummaged in the bottom of an old suitcase. Yes, it was still there! Now, where would be the best place? His mind ranged over several possibilities, and finally he hit on the one that was exactly right.

The next few days, he was very busy and his family were intrigued. On the third day, Simon arrived home from work earlier than usual, while it was still daylight. He took his gun from his case upstairs, loaded it and put the spare bullets in his coat pocket. He then put on a cap and hid a scarf of Maud's in the pocket as well. He then quietly left the house.

Not far away from his house there was a busy little shop that sold everything. He remembered where the owner usually stood behind the counter, and what was in the shelf above her.

When Simon got near the shop, he paused and tied the scarf clumsily over his lower face, went in and said, 'Hands up or I'll shoot,' in his most ferocious voice.

The woman was terrified.

'Open the till and give me the money,' Simon ordered.

She hastened to obey, standing just underneath the large tins of tomato juice. The woman pushed the money towards Simon, who thrust it into his pocket, then took aim, and the woman screamed loudly as she realised he was going to kill her. Simon fired the revolver twice. The woman crashed to the ground, and the punctured tins of tomato juice poured down upon her. Simon left the shop unhurriedly, and as the shop owner, coming to from her faint, saw all the thick red sticky liquid covering her, screamed again in a series of penetrating and ear-splitting shrieks that carried for a great distance. People rushed to her assistance.

Simon was arrested the same afternoon. He pleaded guilty. When his trial eventually came up, he pleaded guilty again, and said that he was only sorry that he hit the tomato juice – his aim was off – as he had fully intended to finish off the fat old woman completely. The jury thought he was a cold-blooded killer and no mistake. The verdict was no surprise. He got life.

*

Six months later, Simon, sitting comfortably reading in his cell, wondered what he would do today. There was a good show on telly that he thought he would watch, or, perhaps he might finish the interesting novel he had borrowed from the library. He stretched luxuriously; nothing really had to be done and, most importantly of all, no one would ever ask him what was his opinion on anything ever again!

He did what he was told to do without expressing an opinion on the work; ate what he was given, without saying what he thought of the food; was agreeable to everyone and everyone liked him.

The only fear that sometimes depressed him, was the thought that, being such a model prisoner, they might, through misguided sentiment, grant him an early release. But really, even on that subject, he had no real opinion on the matter, one way or the other. Simon had achieved his Nirvana: he had no opinions whatsoever now on anything.

A Fishy Story

'There you are,' Betty the barmaid smiled, as she placed the metal container on the bar. 'Want anything else?'

The traveller hesitated. He then asked, 'Could I please have a whisky chaser, if it's not too much trouble?'

'No trouble at all,' Betty assured this diffident customer – he was obviously from Upside; those from Downside were never as polite as this! With a flick of her tail, she dashed to the rows of bottles securely fixed to the shelf, poured the required dram and, with another flash of glittering silver scales, was back to her customer.

'There, get that down inside you and you'll feel much better,' she added with a confidential wink. 'It's all a bit strange at first, but you quickly get used to it.'

'Please, I didn't mean to stare. It was very rude but,' the man broke off, a blush turning the water round his head a pinkish colour, 'I've never seen a mermaid before.'

Betty laughed. 'Lord love you! I'm no mermaid! Just because I've got a tail instead of legs doesn't mean I'm a mermaid. I'm a human, just like you. I know,' she suddenly declared as she glanced at the man's legs, 'you've only just arrived, haven't you?'

'Well, I have, that's true. It's all rather baffling. You see, I was standing on the sand of our little island and suddenly the water kept rising and rising. Before I realised it, the water was over my head, but I was still breathing – it didn't make sense.'

'I understand perfectly,' Betty replied. 'Virtually the same thing happened to us. On our island – this pub stood forty feet higher than the ocean, and in less than ten minutes, we were under the ocean – they said, at the time it was Global Warming, you see.'

'Goodness me!' gasped the newcomer. 'Fancy that! Forty feet Upside and suddenly gone Downside! How did you cope?'

'Well, I have to admit it was difficult at first. I think for the first two weeks, I cried and cried. You see, I had very beautiful legs – even if I do say so myself – and to see them turning into a tail was a shock. You'd have to agree it was a shock.'

The new arrival, blushed again – he was very young. 'If I may say so, Miss, I think your new tail is very beautiful, just like shimmering silver …' He paused and added, 'My name's Abel.'

Betty was delighted to hear the compliment. She moved closer to the bar. 'My name's Betty. I do hope you like our pub and continue to come here whenever you feel like a drink.' She paused to fix her long and beautiful hair. 'I think I met your brother once. If I remember rightly, he came to a bad end.'

The shy young man smiled. 'Betty, I'm most certainly coming here again, but you're right about my brother – I'm sorry you met him. The only thing he ever achieved was to leave his mark on some people.' Abel sat up straight and looked squarely at Betty. 'Please, Betty, if you're not too busy at the moment, would you answer some questions?'

'Of course, Abel. Nothing much to do at the moment. I'll just swab down the bar while we're talking, so fire away.' Betty stayed close to Abel as she scrubbed at difficult spots on the bar with seaweed and then used a sea sponge to clean the area thoroughly.

'How come, Betty, that I can breathe here, under the water?' he asked.

'That's easy, Abel,' she answered. 'Just feel under your armpits. Do you notice anything different?'

The young man hurriedly put one hand under his armpit. His face registered amazement. 'Betty, what's happened to me?' he asked fearfully.

'Nothing to worry about, love. You've just grown gills, that's all.'

'Grown gills, already?'

'Yes, that's another lie they told us. You know about evolution taking millions and millions of years to mutate into something else? It takes exactly eleven seconds for a human being to grow gills.' Betty began to chuckle. 'And it's just as well that's so, otherwise we'd be in a pretty kettle of… Oh, dear, I nearly used the forbidden expression! You know what I mean.'

Abel realised that that could cause a problem, in that particular environment, so hurried on to the next question. 'Well, now I have gills, Betty, does this mean that I, too, will grow a tail?'

'Of course you will, ducky!' Betty assured Abel. 'You'd have a damned hard time getting around Downside without one.'

'Does it hurt much? I've always been a bit of a squib with anything medical. I'm dreading some sort of amputation.'

Betty laughed loudly. 'Lord you're an innocent, aren't you, Abel? There's no operation. It's all done by what they call evolution. It only takes a couple of weeks. The legs join together and you find you've got a tail.' Betty looked at her customer. 'Abel, you're a tall fellow with a good physique, so I think you're going to look pretty grand with a long tail.'

'I'm glad you think so, Betty. I find the whole thing very scary. I'm also angry about it all. After all, I didn't ask to come down here. I was just walking my dog – I did love my dog – along the beach, minding my own business, and here I am – being turned into a merman.' Abel paused and rubbed his nose absent-mindedly with a jelly blubber which happened to be passing. There was an indignant hiss, and the creature was off like a rocket.

'Here, Abel, be careful of what you touch, Downside,' warned Betty. 'That fellow can turn nasty…'

'Well, that's what I mean,' complained Abel. 'How do I know who's friendly and who isn't?'

'Yes, it's tricky. I'm fortunate. I work on the principle that if they come in here for a drink, they don't mind us as interlopers. It's the ones who don't come in that scare me.'

'Such as?'

'Well, I've never seen a white pointer in here asking for a nightcap – and they never sleep, so you'd think they'd need one occasionally. And then there's the swordfish and the giant squid – don't care much for them.

But, really, on the whole, most of the others are fairly friendly, and that's pretty tolerant when you think about it – after all, this is their land, not ours. Some have even welcomed us – not the lobsters, though. They're still carrying a grudge – they turn red at the sight of us.'

'But everything floats so alarmingly,' protested Abel. 'I see you've had to fasten all the bottles down and use the heavy drinking mugs.'

'Yes, that's true, but you must admit that it's a damn sight easier than walking, and lifting things now is a dream. In our line of work, you often have to lift heavy barrels. That used to be a problem for me, now it's a breeze.' Betty leaned over the bar and squeezed Abel's hand. 'Look, love, you'll soon get used to it.'

'But whose fault is it that we're here at all, Betty? I've always done my duty and voted at election time, and each government promised this would never happen. Some even said Global Warning was a load of rubbish, said it wasn't true and sea levels would never rise.'

'And they were right!'

'What?'

'I said the politicians were right. It had nothing to do with Global Warming, or carbon emissions, or any man-made thing…'

'Well, whose fault was it then?'

'Why, King Neptune's of course!' answered Betty, surprised Abel didn't know.

'You're joking!'

'I'm not, you know. King Neptune rules the sea and all in it. It was he who decided enough was enough, so he puffed out his fat cheeks and blew the seas into a tumult which covered a great deal of the lower regions of the earth.'

'But, Betty, Neptune is a…myth…' Abel was startled by Betty frantically putting her hand over his mouth.

'Don't, Abel! Not another word.' Betty leaned closer and whispered: 'He's got his spies everywhere. Look at that barramundi having a sherry at the end of the bar – he's a spy. And that octopus – they've got their tentacles into everything.'

Abel was listening to Betty in astonishment. So he had landed in a police state! 'Betty, is there no way out? You know, back to Upside?'

'Not until the seas go down and that won't happen until His Majesty is satisfied that sea horses will be classified properly Upside. That was the reason he acted.'

'Classified properly, Betty? What do you mean?'

'Well, you know, classified as equine, not as marine creatures. Makes sense, really, for they are horses, aren't they?' Abel agreed. The logic was indisputable.

Suddenly he had an idea. 'Betty, what if you and I – once my tail has grown – were to escape to Upside and tell the authorities about the situation. All they would have to do is reclassify sea horses and all the Downsiders would have their homes back again.'

Betty looked unconvinced. 'It's a lovely idea, Abel, but I'm not all that keen on going Upside just yet. I had a nasty experience last time I went for a quiet swim out of the protected zone.'

'Why? What happened?'

'Well, firstly you have to realise something, Abel. Upsiders now are our enemies, and the worst of them are the professional fishermen. Only a month ago I went too near the surface of the ocean and a dreadful thing happened: I was hooked! It was very embarrassing; I was dragged into their disgusting boat. I had fish in my hair, crabs entangled in my blouse... Oh! It was awful!'

'What did the fishermen do when they saw what they'd caught?' Abel realised that that was an indelicate question, so quickly added, 'That is, Betty, if it's right to ask such a question of a lady.'

'No, that part was all right. The problem was, they treated me as though I were a freak. They made me sit on a special seat and took photos of me and pretended that they couldn't understand one word I was saying. I couldn't really understand them much either – of course they were Scotsmen from the Highlands, so they could have been speaking English, one would never know. However, I did understand that they intended putting me in an aquarium, and people would pay money to come and see the freak from the sea. When they weren't looking, I slid to the side of the boat, dived over and swam quickly back home.' Betty started to cry, 'I'm not a freak, Abel. I'm just an ordinary girl.'

Abel, who was beginning to feel strange about the knees and ankles, hurried round the bar to comfort the weeping girl. 'I think those men were despicable!' he cried and took the fish/girl into his arms.

'You're a good kind man, Abel. Thank you. I'll be all right now. It just upsets me to think of what it used to be like… But Abel,' Betty stopped speaking and was staring at Abel in astonishment. 'What's happening? You're changing before my eyes – this is the quickest change I've ever seen.'

Abel didn't have time to answer; he twisted several ways in a corkscrew manner and grimaced several times in some pain, but very soon moved back to his side of the bar, unaware that he had got there with a simple swish of his long and very handsome tail. Betty actually clapped her hands in delight as she beheld the merman standing before her.

Abel, seeing his reflection in the mirror behind the bar, felt his nervousness and shyness disappear; he was aware he looked really cool – dashing, in fact. He took Betty's hand. 'Betty, I feel as if nothing can stop us now. You and I will go Upside and convince those idiots to do what the king ordered and the world can be turned right side up once again.' He thrust out his chest. 'We will go in the king's name!'

Betty cried with joy and pride, and took the hand held out to her. She and Abel plighted their troth and prepared for the big adventure.

It took ten days to get ready. Betty had to give a week's notice in order to get her holiday pay, and her rightful share of the tips, while Abel was busy about the king's work. However, when all the preparations were complete, they stood ready, side by side.

As they took their places, Abel held the king's warrant in his right hand and Betty's hand in his left. They waited until there was a drum roll from stage left; then on the cue from the stage director, both Betty and Abel raised their heads proudly. A submerged orchestra – it was the Royal Philharmonic – began to play the last section of the triumphant march from *Aida* as the young couple slowly rose from the depths – between the royal guard of one thousand and seven sea horses – to the rosy glow from the setting sun, which penetrated deep into the ocean. They were like two heroic figures from an ancient Norse legend – heroic, invincible, saviours of their people. The last triumphant chord sounded as their heads broke the surface of the sea. Victory was within their grasp; the submerged world would now be saved! Sea horses would once again take their rightful place in history!

Urgent correction:

I'm sorry to have to interrupt this movie-like ending to this story, but the truth is: it's simply not true! Betty and Abel achieved nothing! As soon as Betty and Abel reached the surface, they were entangled in a fisherman's net, processed and were being served, along with chips – and, in the more expensive places, a side salad – Upside, in restaurants, the very next day!

A Hand in Need…

Professor Vladimir Holdemoffacov, his hands moving at the speed of light, finished the piano concerto in a dazzling glissando that made his listeners gasp. There was a moment's silence in the vast auditorium, then the audience leapt to their feet, cheering and clapping for seven minutes. The maestro and the conductor took thirteen bows altogether. The critics were writing shorthand at great speed – superlatives shooting off at a tremendous rate – then dashing off to meet deadlines, while the great man wiped his forehead with a gleaming white handkerchief before finally leaving the stage for the silence and peace of his dressing room.

Inside the dressing room, his manager-cum-valet-cum-gopher and general factotum, spoke timidly to his exalted employer. 'Another glorious achievement, maestro…' only to be shushed by a hand held up like a traffic warden.

Fred Browlow was used to his boss, so held his tongue and waited for instructions, which he knew would be coming. He also knew what these instructions would be: warnings to the reporters to follow the rules the maestro set down or the interviews would finish immediately. Fred was correct; it was all as usual.

'About the reporters,' the professor said, coldly. 'I refuse to allow any of them to come nearer to me than six feet three inches. They are to speak only when I give them the nod. They will confine themselves only to questions about my musical performance, and I refuse utterly to answer one single question about my private life. Music,' he repeated, 'they must only ask about music. And remember, definitely no autographs, none whatsoever, and don't forget, I refuse to permit them to touch me in any way – they must not touch me!'

The ever-diplomatic Fred raised his hands in a placating manner. 'You know you have no worries with me handling all that, sir. The reporters understand your requirements and are very respectful – as of course they should be with the greatest pianist in the whole world who is able to play a four-hand concerto with only two hands. They adore you.'

The maestro pulled a sour face, but Fred was used to that also. The public might adore you, Fred thought, but I think you're a big pain in the…

He was saved from thinking further as they came out into the corridor and found a group of pressmen and women waiting. Fred immediately moved in front of his boss and laid down the rules of engagement. The reporters understood and stepped back the required distance. The professor dabbed at his face with his large white handkerchief and then nodded to one of the men.

'Sir,' asked the reporter, 'would you tell the world the secret of the speed of your brilliant playing…' He got not further.

'Genius,' was the terse reply.

The same reporter tried again. 'But no other pianist in the world can handle what you do. There has to be an explanation…what is it?'

'Practice.'

A pretty press woman from *Music World* journal was the next to try. 'But, maestro, you can handle the very difficult to play chords of Liszt without any difficulty. How do you do it? I mean, nearly every other pianist in the world has great difficulty with them, yet you do them with ease, and at such speed! How can you explain that?'

'I am unique.'

The professor was beginning to show signs familiar to Fred. He knew he had to stop the questions soon or it would cause all sorts of problems. He was just about to make an excuse and edge the maestro away, when the girl reporter screamed.

Everyone turned to look at the girl, who was staring at the professor's shirt front. The girl was frightened and shouted, hysterically, 'He's got another hand. It's scratching his belly.'

Everyone then fixed their eyes on the pianist.

He, in turn, began scratching at his chest himself, and angrily turned his wrath on Fred. 'Fleas!' he screamed hysterically. 'Give notice to the management immediately. I leave this filthy barn tonight. I will not play in any place that cannot keep vermin from it.'

Fred was aghast. How was he going to handle this? The building was the concert hall of the Royal Opera House in Vienna. To accuse the management of fleas was unthinkable; if he couldn't talk the idiot out of breaking his contract here, he'd have to think up another more plausible excuse than fleas! Meanwhile, he tried to defuse the situation.

He raised his eyebrows at the reporters, humorously, and hustled the maestro back down the corridor, and into his dressing room. He went to speak to Holdemoffacov but received a stream of abuse, and was told to get out and wait until he was called for. As Fred left the room, he thought he saw what was, of course, impossible. He actually thought he saw the professor unscrew his own hand and place it on the dressing room table, and then – horror of horrors – the hand began to talk!

Fred hurried from the room, his face white. He was obviously losing his mind; he was now seeing things. No wonder: he had been with the professor for three years now and everyone knew this weird goat was enough to send anyone round the bend.

Outside in the corridor, Fred heard the woman reporter say to her colleagues. 'Now, don't ask me anything about it. I know it's impossible, but I also know what I saw. And I'm warning you – all of you – if you dare ask me am I sure that I saw it, I'll belt you over the ear. I know what I saw, and I saw a hand. I can't understand it, but I can't explain it away either.'

With that, she turned on her heel and walked rapidly away, her colleagues following her speaking quietly and worriedly. Erica had always been a stable woman; what on earth had gone wrong with her? She wasn't on the drink again, was she?

While waiting for the professor to call him when he wanted something done, Fred considered his options. He could leave this weirdo, but then, remembering the contract he had signed when he first obtained the job, he'd then have to pay one million dollars. The professor had made that a condition for accepting the position. He also remembered the reason why he, out of all those who applied, was chosen: it was because he actually resembled the professor in looks – the professor had said he only liked looking at people who actually looked like him.

As Fred's hair was fair, and the professor's black, Fred – in order to get the job – had dyed his hair black. The professor was satisfied. Now, they really did look alike. Of course, Fred was a realist, and knew he had made good money working for this bloke, but losing a million? No way, after what he had had to put up with during the past three years: the fads, the fantasies, the food that he wouldn't touch; the foods that he must have or he would die; the stupid, solitary life he lived, refusing to associate even with his fellow musicians. And then his peculiarities when travelling! Who ever heard of anyone travelling with a fresh supply of pickled water everywhere he went? Mad! The man might be a genius, but he was stark raving bonkers as far as Fred was concerned.

Fred was understandably miserably aware that, if he didn't want to end up penniless, he was stuck with the maestro; he'd just have to make the best of it. He smiled crookedly, remembering how thrilled he had been getting the job; he had vainly imagined that it would help him in his own dream of becoming a concert pianist himself. What a joke! He had certainly trained for years, but he knew he never had what it really takes, and anyhow, the professor had made it clear that no one but he would ever play the piano while Fred was in his employ; he could not tolerate hearing anyone else play, so Fred's career came to an end.

Fred glanced at his watch. What the hell was the man doing in there, he wondered. He wanted his supper and, no matter the consequences, he made the decision to knock on the door if it didn't open in another minute.

It was just as well for Fred's sanity that he didn't know what Vladimir was doing, or it is possible he could have died from fright.

*

The professor was talking to a hand which was lying on his dressing table; and the hand was talking back!

The maestro was angry, and letting the hand know it. 'You were nothing, and I made you the Hand of Glory, you ungrateful thing!' he snapped.

'Yes, I became the Hand of Glory – I'm not complaining about that, although I would never have agreed, had I known it would entail so much work, and so much damn boring music. But how dare you insinuate that you would have been anything else than a second-rate run of the mill pianist, had I not made you the celebrity you are now.'

'I could have reached the heights without you…'

'Oh yeah? You couldn't even play the chords in Liszt's works, let alone handle four-hand pieces with only two hands. It was that, you dumb clown, which made you the talk of the world, nothing else. And I made that possible.' The hand paused and then continued, 'But it's all coming to an end now…'

The maestro interrupted frantically. 'What do you mean? It can't come to an end! Remember our agreement when I dug up the body and cut you off from the corpse? You promised to stay with me forever, and I've done everything you asked. I've even carried that blasted embalming fluid around with me everywhere I went, having to pretend it's pickled water and having to cope with all the looks and complaints of the smell. What more could I have done for you?'

'You could have taken me to some places I wanted to see, not just the places you wanted.'

'We've been everywhere…

'Oh no, we haven't.'

The maestro became exasperated. 'Well, where the hell do you want to go, you ungrateful, selfish thing?'

'Back.'

'What do you mean, back? Back where?'

'To my body. I miss it. I want to be whole again. You must take me back. You have no option. I'll come out and tell the world about what you did, if you won't. I nearly did it tonight with that nice-looking girl, but I decided to give you one more chance.'

The pianist fell silent, pondering deeply the situation; he was aware how deadly serious it was. He shuddered at the thought that he could be exposed to the whole world as a complete fraud. Perhaps it was time to put the hand back; he'd certainly have enough money to live on for the rest of his days, and, more importantly, he could retire now in a burst of glory. But he'd try to bargain a bit – this thing was not going to have the last word!

'All right, you win. I'll take you back to yourself. But first, I want you to agree to two more televised concerts at the Albert Hall. Then I'll announce my retirement.'

'No! I refuse utterly to do two. I'll do one. One only! Get that clear in your head.'

The professor sighed. 'One it is then. Let's shake on it. It's a deal – one more concert and then back you go. Satisfied?'

'No, 'cause you're tricky, but it'll have to do. I'll be watching you all the time, remember that…and I notice that your hand is sweating. That's a bad sign. I suggest you take some aspirin to settle down.'

The professor made an exasperated sound, grabbed the hand, thrust it into its bottle of fluid and screwed down the lid. When the bottle was hidden from sight, he sent for his manager to arrange the televised concert.

*

The televised concert went off with a bang. Everyone who was anyone was there. It was a gala night. The word had got about that the brilliant pianist was about to retire and the hall was packed; people stood in the aisles. The cheering at the end nearly lifted the roof. The professor took fifteen curtain calls, and could have taken more, had not the hand threatened him that, if he didn't leave the stage immediately, he would come out of hiding and tell all. Vladimir left quickly.

Fred was mystified by the instructions he had received. He had the limousine waiting for the maestro, as ordered, at the hall door, but couldn't understand why his employer insisted on driving himself, telling his manager that he would not need him again that night. Fred was intrigued. Where the devil was the man going? Was it an assignation? If it were, it would be the first in three years, as far as Fred knew. And why was it all so secret? There and then, Fred decided to follow the professor and get to the bottom of the mystery.

In a car Fred had rented, he followed the maestro out of the city and into the country. This was odd. Fred knew that the professor hated the country. Even more extraordinary, Vladimir's car came to a halt in a little road fronting a remote and secluded cemetery. There was only a little moon and Fred was able to creep closely behind his boss, and found himself only one tombstone away from him, when he stopped dead and began to shake with fear at what he saw.

The maestro had thrown off his coat and, taking a hand from a pocket, had thrown it, with the coat, unknowingly, at the feet of his manager. He then took a spade, which he had been shielding with his coat, and began to dig into the grave. Fred drew in his breath and held it; he was petrified. What on earth possessed the man? Had he gone completely mad? Was he secretly some kind of grave robber?

When Vladimir reached the coffin, the sound of the spade opening it, went screeching into the black, night air. As if poor Fred's nerves were not jangled enough, it was at that moment that the hand spoke!

'Well, go on you nincompoop,' he jeered. 'Afraid of what you're going to see? You should have thought of that before. Hey, what are you staring at like that? What's wrong?'

'There nothing left,' the professor managed to stutter in disbelief.

'Nothing left? Let me see.' The hand suddenly bounced across the grass and stood at the side of the grave. It let out a yell. 'I've been robbed, that's what happened.' The hand leapt quickly at the professor's throat, and began to throttle him. 'You wicked beast, you've robbed me of me. There's only this hand left. Well, I've got to have a body. Yours will do.'

After a final hideous tussle, the professor gave a long sigh, and slid down onto the wet grass; he was quite dead.

Fred thought he was in the middle of a nightmare. This couldn't be real, could it? He would just get into the car and go away; he would pretend he hadn't seen anything; no one would believe him if he said that a hand had murdered the great man. He'd... His eyes suddenly nearly popped out of his head and he shook violently in terror.

Fred saw the hand pluck a saw from somewhere. It was neatly sawing off the hand of the professor, muttering as he did so, 'I need a body and this one is the only one available, so sorry, old chap, and all that, but you were a frightful bore to be with for the last three years.' With the hand severed, he threw the professor's hand over near Fred and, dragging the body of the maestro to the edge of the grave, tipped it into the coffin. When that was done, the hand jumped in at the last moment, and pulled the lid down.

Fred looked down at the hand. He was aware of two things: this was the explanation of the maestro's extraordinary brilliance; it had nothing to do with his own genius, the sneaking cheat! He also understood, for the first time, about the Hand of Glory; he had thought it was all poppycock, now he knew it was actually true.

The reality of his situation then hit him; he was alone in a churchyard with a dead hand! A sudden fear began hammering at his brain: he had to get rid of this thing, somehow. Perhaps the river? There was a bridge close to the cemetery; he'd drop it over the side. By the time anyone found it, they would never know to whom it belonged. With trembling fingers, Fred picked up the hand in his handkerchief, wrapped it in his long scarf, and began to make his way to the bridge on foot; it was not far away.

As he walked with his burden, he began to wonder about the hand. I suppose, he thought, this new hand from the professor was also now a Hand of Glory which, they say, could do wonders. Well, the other one certainly did extraordinary things for the professor – the wealth, the celebrity status, the luxurious lifestyle.

He wondered, if... No, he'd never be able to pull it off...or could he? After all, they did look alike...and he did study music all those years... and...he did know the pieces the professor played. But, no, he couldn't, but with the Hand of Glory, who would be able to stop him now? Could he do it? Well, it was possible he could do it, as it wouldn't actually be him doing it at all…would it?

Fred carefully put the hand down and went back to the open grave. He climbed down into the grave, opened it and searched the professor's clothing, taking his wallet and all the maestro's keys. He then climbed back, took the spade, filled in the grave and carefully tidied up around the area. He then threw the spade into the bushes. He decided, then and there, to drive his car back to the rental place, steal a bicycle, ride back, and throw the bike away before driving back, in style, to the hotel in the professor's limousine. Well, it was fitting, wasn't it? He now was the maestro! Nothing could ever stop him now!

With reverence, Fred stooped and picked up the hand in the scarf. Slowly, very slowly, he unwrapped it. He quickly leapt back in terror; the hand had immediately gone for his throat! Fred attempted to scream as he staggered about the moonlit cemetery trying desperately to release the iron grip, but only a hideous gurgle came forth from his gaping mouth, while his eyeballs stood out of his head like a gargoyle's. Moving backward, he tripped over a tombstone and fell heavily. He never regained his feet. He fought with all his might, but it was useless; his struggles slowly began to weaken, his whole body convulsed twice, then all movement ceased completely.

The pale moon was the only witness to the sight of a single hand scrabbling at the dirt on a newly filled grave, trying frantically to move the soil to rejoin his body, while sobbing inconsolably. Eventually it, too, ceased to struggle, panted dreadfully, then lay still.

As the moon entered the last phase of the night, the hand had become a withered skeleton, while the corpse of the murdered manager, Fred Browlow, lay staring sightlessly up at the morning star.

The next morning, the police were alerted by the vicar. The body was easily identified – by the wallet and personal keys – as the great musician, Professor Vladimir Holdemoffacov. It was instantly assumed that his missing manager, Fred Browlow, was the murderer and a wide-ranging police hunt was put in place to catch the dreaded killer. Needless to say, it was not successful. The remains of a human hand the police ignored, declaring that a stray dog must have dug it up from one of the graves. They hesitated a little, wondering what to do with it, but an enterprising young copper, by the name of Edgerton Smythe-Bickerton – commonly known as Pongo, removed it from one of the police dogs' mouths and threw the Hand of Glory, negligently, without thinking, into an incinerator.

The professor – in reality, Fred Browlow – received a state funeral with all the pomp and ceremony due to a great artist, while Vladimir Holdemoffacov remained in a damp cemetery. Without any ceremony at all.

Is There Anyone There?

Seven men and women sat around the table. They had joined their hands and were watching the medium, Mrs Gladys Snipe, with a mixture of fear and excited apprehension. The medium had a tremendous reputation, yet her manner seemed odd at first – she was so ordinary, so commonplace.

She had spoken generally for the first ten minutes discussing the difficulty of getting a decent perm anywhere these days with the modern fetish for straight, lank hair, the outrageous price of pantihose, the worming of her dog and the need to get her cat desexed. It was a shock then, when she suddenly threw her head back, and began to breathe through the mouth, in a loud and stertorious manner. The room immediately became freezing cold; the guests were frightened and shivered delightedly, filled with fearful expectation, goosebumps and excitement.

This awful breathing noise of the medium continued for the next few minutes, then she spoke in a flat, metallic voice. 'Is there anyone there?'

There was silence in the room for a moment or two, then the trance-like calm was shattered by a loud and vulgar voice replying, 'Of course there is, and you know it, you charlatan! It's Mrs McCuddy, your landlady.'

The guests around the table were bewildered and glanced quickly at each other, unsure whether this was a spirit or a real human being speaking.

However, the strange, calm voice of the medium continued as before, not the slightest bit perturbed. 'Do you have a message, Mrs McCuddy, for anyone here?'

'Of course I have: get home before you lose any more money from this crook.'

'I mean, dear spirit guide, any specific message from someone who has passed over?'

'Passed over what? I've told you before to stop using that ridiculous phrase. I certainly passed over the bridge to get here tonight – the traffic was terrible.' There was an irritated sigh, and then the voice continued, 'My message is dead easy: I want my rent money, and if it's not collected now, someone here who owns a brand-new Audi will find, when he leaves this house tonight, that it has been keyed all along both sides.' There followed a burst of bawdy laughter.

The medium remained unperturbed. It seemed that she did not see anything at all peculiar with this conversation. 'Now, McCuddy, you'll get your rent money. There's no need for you to insult our guests…'

'Our guests! They're not *our* guests, they're yours. I wouldn't associate with a bunch of morons like these! They'd swallow your baloney any day of the week but they don't fool me. You'd better fork over the rent now, or I'm warning you, there'll be trouble – especially for the Audi owner.' Another burst of raucous laughter, after which it said, 'Send round the hat.'

The medium's head came forward; she looked at the seated people and spoke in her normal voice. 'Our control is in a bad mood. We'd better humour her. You never know with Elsa McCuddy: she has a wicked sense of humour.'

A shining, unattached, hand appeared and handed round a bag in which people hurriedly placed whatever money they could grab quickly. The money when collected disappeared from the table mysteriously, while the medium, slipping easily back into her trance, spoke again.

'Now, Elsa…'

'Who said you could call me Elsa? It's Mrs McCuddy to you while ever you're living in my house, which I don't think will be for much longer, if I can help it.'

'Mrs McCuddy, is there any other spirit there that wants to speak to us?'

'So I see I'm now not good enough for you, is that it? Let me remind you I've had offers from other mediums who are much better than you are. Regarding this lot of dupes, I had a couple of messages, but if you don't appreciate what I'm doing, then you can go hang – which anyone in their right mind would have done with you years ago. I'm off.'

The medium jerked herself forward again and spoke quickly to the group. 'Quickly, we can't lose her. Often money sweetens her up. Send round the bag again and see if that will pacify her.'

The bag materialised again, and went the rounds of the table at the speed of light; it disappeared again equally fast.

'Mrs McCuddy, are you still there?'

'Of course I'm still here. I'd be a fool to go away when these idiots are throwing money at me. What do you want?'

'How kind of you to stay, dear Mrs…'

'You can cut that out straight away. I know you through and through. You'll get nothing from me with your hypocritical sweet talk.'

'Mrs McCuddy, please pay attention. Are there any messages from the other side for my friends here?'

'I have a couple…' muttered the voice reluctantly.

'From the ether?'

'Don't be ridiculous! I got a text message from a friend of mine who works in the newsroom of the radio station.'

The medium gave a long and weary sigh. She obviously was well used to dealing with this difficult spirit. 'Would you please get on with it, and tell us what they are?'

'Only if there is an Alison Gray present. I have a message for an Alison Gray.'

One of the women seated at the table held up her trembling hand. 'I'm Alison Gray,' she whispered.

'Good grief! You're as ugly as your mother! No wonder you're into this racket. Well, the message for you could be either good, or bad, depending on how much money you owe.' Another burst of horrible laughter. 'The bad news is, your mother is dead, but all the money is now yours – so it could be good news.'

There was a cry of grief from the girl at the table.

The medium went on, 'Is Alison's mother happy on the other side?'

'How the hell do I know? I don't go round asking people if they're happy or not.'

'Couldn't you tell from looking at her?'

'How could I bear to look at her? I've told you she was…'

'Yes, well, never mind that. Let's leave that, Mrs McCuddy. About the money…did the poor soul have any advice for Alison about that?'

'Apart from giving me one half of it, she was free to do whatever she wanted with the rest of it.'

'It wouldn't have come to much, would it?'

'And you call yourself a medium? You're an idiot, or else a very wealthy woman, if you don't think twenty million is much. If that's the case, I want my back rent as well as all moneys owing to me, as well as the money for the broken locks on the cupboards in the kitchen.'

The medium ignored these personal requests and continued, 'The second message, Mrs McCuddy? Who was that for?'

'Just hold your horses, woman. Has that Gray woman signed over half her money to me yet?'

'That's all been done, dear. Now, the second message, please.'

'It's for a John Smith. Is that dope there among the group of the gullible seven?'

'Dear Mr Smith is a regular attender, Mrs McCuddy. Of course he's here.'

'More fool him! More fool him! Well, tell the idiot that he's just won the jackpot lottery. It went up to twenty-five million this time.'

The man jumped up from the table with a loud cry of joy. 'At last! After all these years, and everyone telling me that I was wasting my money buying lottery tickets! Oh, twenty-five million!'

'Tell that fool to sit down, Mrs Snipe. I haven't finished.'

John Smith sat down quickly.

The voice continued, 'I forgot to ask if his middle name was Eustace: that's the John Smith who won the prize.'

There was another cry from John Smith, this time of anguish and despair. 'No! It isn't! I can't believe this is happening to me. My second name is Albert.'

'Then it's not you, is it?' There was another burst of laughter. 'Better luck next time, but what the odds would be of a John Smith winning twice in a row won't bear thinking about, will it?'

'Mrs McCuddy, that was not kind, not kind at all. I'm going to leave you now. If you can't behave in a polite manner when I have guests in, then I'll have to get another spirit who has a kind nature.'

'You'll be lucky. We're in such short demand now, we can charge anything we like. I think you'll be stuck with me for a long time to come.'

The medium was seen to shudder, then appeared to convulse, and sat up, her eyes blinking and looking confused. She looked around the table. 'Did it go all right? You understand I have no idea whether it was successful or not. I cannot promise anything as I never know what will happen. Did we get a spirit? Were there messages from the other side?'

The seven people quickly filled in the medium with what had happened, paid their fee, then quietly left the room, Mrs Snipe looking bewildered at Alison Gray, weeping sadly into a handkerchief as she joined the others.

*

With the departure of the guests, Gladys Snipe stretched out her legs and leant back in her chair. She turned the lights up and called out to her assistant, 'Put the kettle on, Elsa, I'm completely done in.'

As a tall, angular woman entered the room with a late supper on a tray, Gladys wearily declared, 'It fair takes it out of me, it does. It's not easy, dear, let me tell you.'

Elsa was sympathetic. 'I know, dear, but we did all right tonight, although I was worried about the temperature. I think I turned the freezer down too low when I opened the door. However, on the bright side, Alison's share of the money will be a windfall and no mistake. Where will we go this time?'

Gladys became thoughtful. 'I'm not sure, but definitely not Transylvania. I never want to even hear about spirits, séances or anything

58

to do with any of it for the next six months – or until the money runs out. OK?'

Elsa smiled. 'OK by me, Gladys. I find it all pretty exhausting myself, especially when you go off the script as you do so often.'

'What about you? You and that John Eustace Smith business! I didn't know what to do. I nearly burst out laughing.'

'Well, I get bored with the same old lines. I like to be a bit creative. Now let's forget business and have supper, and watch a good western on the box. What do you say?'

'Just what I need! A bit of good make-believe is just what the doctor ordered.'

The two middled-aged fraudsters sat comfortably in front of the fire, and ate their supper of cheese on toast happily, with the satisfaction of a job well done.

The women suddenly felt the room turn freezing cold; a clap of thunder rattled a non-existent door in the middle of the fireplace, while a low keening sound circled around them. Gladys and Elsa were paralysed with fear; they clung to each other terrified.

Eventually, with quavering voices they asked nervously, 'Is there anyone there?'

The Last Patient

Dr L. Screw breathed a sigh of relief. The last candidate for her temporary replacement had arrived and stood at the door of her consulting rooms. The psychiatrist could hardly wait for this afternoon to be over; she would then be on holidays for a whole three weeks. She hated these interviews and was heartily sick of the same questions with usually the same answers. However, it was a formality and, though it bored her to tears, she just had to get on with it. The director had demanded the screening of the doctors, in case there was the slightest possibility that they could be mentally disturbed. He had blathered on about the necessity for a psychiatrist to be a perfectly normal, sane person. Dr Screw yawned when she heard this demand; as if any of the candidates would be crackers! Everyone knew they were supposed to be normal! That was taken for granted.

So far it had been – as she had thought – utterly boring: no one had evinced the slightest abnormality; they were monotonously normal.

Well, only one more to go, she thought with relief, then it's off home for a vacation! What a wonderful word, vacation! During that time, I won't have to pretend to be interested in anyone's damn, dreary story; nor listen to any endless complaining.

She put on her professional face and stood to greet the tall, thin, diffident man as he hesitated in the doorway.

'I say, is this the place where I'm supposed to be?'

'If you're Dr Thomas Threadbare, then you are in the right place,' the psychiatrist responded breezily. 'That's the name I have written down here.'

The young man looked relieved. 'Oh good! What's the L for?'

'I beg your pardon?'

'You know – your name: Dr L. Screw.'

'It's hardly your business, is it? As a matter of fact, it's Lucy, but I prefer to be called Luce.'

'Really! Well, everyone to their own fancies, I always say. And you're the psychiatrist? Just fancy that! I knew a Lucy once; she was as mad as a hatter. Any relation? I mean, if you actually are – you being a Screw Luce – and if all the rest of the Screws were also, family get-togethers must be a hoot!'

Dr Screw pulled herself together. This was getting out of hand; she'd have to control this situation quickly – this one was a smart alec. She assumed her frostiest look, pointed at the couch and said brusquely, 'Lie down on the couch.'

Tom Threadbare looked startled, but did as he was bid. The psychiatrist was just about to give another direction, when she was forestalled by the patient.

'What do I do now?' he asked.

Using her soothing, clinical voice, Dr Screw answered, 'You know the drill: just lie back and have a little rest…'

Immediately, a horrendous snore rent the quiet of the room.

Lucy leapt to her feet. 'What on earth are you doing, you foolish chap?' she shouted as she shook the sleeping man roughly.

The man woke up disgruntled. 'I can't help it if I fall asleep quickly. I was having a lovely dream. I'd just started to grow hair all over my body…Oh, it was so wonderful. I was so happy. I've always wanted to be a gorilla.'

Dr Screw's eyes goggled; she had a real nutcase at last. She grabbed her notebook and, all thoughts of boredom gone, began her questions. 'Have you had this dream before?'

'Oh yes, hundreds of times.'

'Can you remember when you had the first dream about gorillas?'

'Easily! It was just before I stole the tray of bananas from the fruit shop, but don't worry, they didn't prosecute. My mother paid the owner, and he took into consideration my age.' He smiled happily. 'That's the reason I don't have a criminal record.'

'How old were you? Can you remember that?'

'Of course I can. I was eighteen months.'

'You were eighteen months old and you ate a whole tray of bananas?'

'That's right. That was the first tray. Mum had some difficulty in keeping up the bananas, but she took a second job to pay for the food, so I didn't miss out.' He laughed easily. 'Just as well she did. I told her I'd throw her from the balcony if she didn't.' The candidate sighed nostalgically. 'We lived on the thirty-fifth floor.'

'Why are you sighing?' the doctor asked sharply.

'I was thinking of my mother. Such a pity! Such a waste! She hanged herself from the ceiling fan in the living room.'

Dr Screw gasped. 'How terrible!'

'It certainly was. You couldn't see the telly at all. It was worse when you turned the fan on.'

Dr Screw shuddered. 'Dr Threadbare, tell me, how long did your mother hang there?'

'What a weird question! She's still hanging there going round, and round, and round. I think she likes it, so I keep the fan going full blast. I have to dodge the feet – she's still got her shoes on.'

Dr Screw felt for the security button under the carpet beneath the desk but couldn't locate it. In desperation, she thought it better to keep the questions going until she could find it. 'Were there any other signs of this weird – I mean unusual – aspiration of yours?'

'The hair. It began to grow everywhere whenever I felt hungry. Now, every time I feel a little hungry, the hair appears firstly on my hands, then my face. If I'm not fed within fifteen minutes, I'm covered in hair,' the candidate replied. Suddenly, his face flushed with excitement. 'I'm feeling a bit peckish now, so you'll most probably see it sprouting any moment.' Tom Threadbare gave a sudden shout. 'Look, Luce! It's starting on my hands and I can feel it on my cheeks.' The patient looked at the doctor quickly. 'Do you have a banana by any chance left over from lunch? It might delay it a bit.'

Luce Screw stared at her patient in horror, and shifted her feet all over the wretched carpet trying to find the security bell. Where the hell was it? This thing…this gorilla man…is a monster! She must get help. She risked another quick look at the man and bit her lips to stop the screaming. His entire face now was covered in hair, his hands likewise, while his body shape had changed dramatically; the clothes burst asunder and lay in heaps of torn scraps on the floor.

'Dr Threadbare, can you hear me?' the doctor asked loudly.

She was answered by a thundering thumping on the chest of the beast which sounded like two bass drums struck at the same time.

Knowing now that she would never find the bell under her desk, Dr Screw tried a desperate dash to the door, only to be picked up like a rag doll, and shaken with great anger, which left her feeling light-headed and limp. The gorilla, seeing the handbag fall open, spied a banana. He dropped Lucy, grabbed the fruit and began to eat it slowly, while a broad grin spread over his hairy mouth.

Lucy gathered her strength and screamed as loudly as she could.

The gorilla looked concerned. He carefully picked up the psychiatrist and placed her on the couch. 'Now, this won't do at all. Just take a few deep breaths and tell me your trouble. I'll just make a few notes.' He sat down at the desk, and even put on the woman's black-rimmed glasses which the psychiatrist used to impress clients.

'Please,' Lucy begged, 'I…'

'I know what you mean, dear, I really do, but you can't.'

'But…'

'Now, I'll get a teensy bit annoyed with you, sugar plum, if you keep saying that word. I told you, you can't.'

'What do you mean? I can't what?'

'Fly, dear. I understand the desire – the urgent, desperate longing – but it's not allowed…'

'I don't think I want to fly, do I? I want…'

'Oh yes, you do! It's a perfectly natural desire, Now, dear, I'm the psychiatrist. I know all about you, and your intense desire – your need – to fly. What you really want is to fly from your window here like a goose going south, but I'm truly sorry. He said it's not permitted.'

'Who said?'

'Now, don't get agitated, dear. It was the director.'

'How would he know what I want and what I don't want, the stupid ignoramus?'

'Well, that's what I thought myself, but don't tell anyone I said that. You have to trust me when I say I do believe you, when you say you can fly, just like a goose…'

'Can I really fly? No one has ever told me I could fly before…'

'Oh dear, Luce, that memory of yours! Everyone here at the clinic knows about your ability to fly.'

'Do they?'

'Of course they do, they've seen you. Now…'

'Please listen to me, doctor! I don't think I want to be like a goose.' Lucy began to cry. 'I just want to go home…'

'And the quickest way would be for you to fly, wouldn't it? The subway is so crowded in the afternoons, isn't it? You're so right, I understand that, but rules are rules.' Dr Threadbare shook his hairy head sadly. 'I'd like to help you but it's not allowed, you know.'

'So the director did say that, did he?'

'Yes, he did. He's a proper pain in the butt, isn't he?'

'He certainly is, Dr Threadbare. If I want to fly, that's got nothing to do with him. It wasn't in my job description that I couldn't fly if I wanted to, was it?' Lucy got up from the couch. 'I'll show him I can fly. I mean, who does he think he is?' Lucy began muttering incoherently about her boss; some things about him being against her from the beginning, and that he'd never even heard of Women's Lib. Well, she decided, she'd show him.

Dr Threadbare didn't move as the psychiatrist gathered her things together and, going to the window, opened it wide, barely glancing at the moving traffic far, far below.

As Lucy hesitated on the windowsill, her eyes cleared for a moment, and she looked puzzled. 'This is what I really want to do, is it, doctor? Fly home?'

'Well, that's what you said. But I did try to stop you, remember?'

'That's true. Thanks, doctor, I'll keep that in mind. Good evening.' With a flash of nylon stockings and the soles of high-heeled shoes, Lucy went head first through the opening.

Dr Threadbare picked up the phone and punched in the numbers for the director. 'It's Tom Threadbare, Bob. It worked like a dream. We got rid of the crazy dame at last. She didn't even notice the false hair and the gorilla outfit I was wearing under the clothes. She's gone, and good riddance.' Tom started to laugh loudly. 'Just wait a minute, Bob, until I get this blasted suit off.'

A few moments later, there was a terrified scream from the psychiatrist's last patient. He grabbed the phone with trembling hands and shouted, 'Bob, quickly...ugh... Please help me...ugh...ugh... Something's happened to me. Bob, I can't...ugh...get the suit off...I've...ugh...ugh... Get me a banana...ugh... I've become...it!'

The Serious Musician

Weasely Led worshipped at the altar of his friend, Percy Playback, whom he considered to be the greatest King of Rock – better than that other Pretender, whom everyone, for some reason or another, admired. But even though he worshipped Percy, he wasn't slow in giving advice, if he thought Percy needed it.

Take the day that changed history, for example. Weasely had arrived early at Percy's garage – they both called it a studio; it sounded more grand – and found his friend standing on a chair with a rope tied around his neck to one of the rafters in the ceiling.

'What on earth are you doing,' Weasley asked, naturally enough. 'Are you composing a new hit?'

'Go away, Weasely,' cried Percy in tones that suggested severe indigestion but were meant to indicate severe depression.

'But what are you doing, for goodness' sake,' protested Weasely. 'You could easily hurt yourself doing that.'

'I'm hanging myself, you oaf! Now go away.'

'No, I won't,' declared Weasely defiantly. 'I'm not going anywhere until you do it correctly.'

'What did you say?' spluttered Percy, hardly able to believe his ears.

'Do it correctly, I said. Now, let me help you.' He climbed up on another chair, and inspected the knot. 'There, you see? You have the knot in the wrong place. Where you have it tied, it won't break your neck, it'll only give you a nasty bruise.' He undid the rope and tied it correctly.

'Now, there's another thing, Percy,' Weasely went on. 'Don't jump yet. You've got the chair wrong. It's back to front.' He bustled forward. 'Here, let me fix it. Now remember when you jump, the back of the chair is easy to kick away. You'll be sure of it then.'

Percy was suddenly staring into space with a strange look in his eyes. 'Come up here, Weasely,' he ordered sharply, 'and quickly, too.'

Weasely got back up on the chair and was surprised to hear his hero say, 'Now, untie me, you clot. I have a symphony to write.'

'Oh, goodness, do you think you should? I always think if you begin something, you should always carry it through. My mum always said…'

'Undo it instantly, you moron, or you'll be dangling from this rope. I've just had a vision of greatness. All is not lost. All is now found.'

Understanding the situation now, and uttering cries of adoration, Weasely hastened to cut Percy down and, as soon as he did so, the genius rushed to his desk and then to his electronic gadgets. Weasely watched in bewilderment as his hero of rock chose one tape, not from his own huge collection of pop music, but one from his mother's collection: Tchaikovsky's *1812 Overture*.

Weasely watched in horror. What was Percy doing? He had never in his life listened to classical music, and he certainly knew Percy hadn't either. It was Percy's greatness that he had achieved fame as a rock star without knowing the slightest thing about music at all! He had an electric guitar, lots of amplification, lighting, and wonderfully strong lungs which enabled him to scream loudly. That had made him a hit. He had been an instant success – an overnight success – though, to be sure, there had been a slide downwards this past year; for two quarters, he had not been in the top ten hits. Perhaps this was the reason Percy had been going to hang himself.

Weasely wondered how he could ask this delicately, but after some deliberation, he steeled himself and went ahead. 'Master, why were you going to top yourself? To pull the plug, as it were?'

Percy looked up briefly. His eyebrows rose. 'Top myself? Don't be ridiculous! I was seeking inspiration.'

'Oh…about a rock symphony?'

'Good gracious, Weasely, don't you know anything? It's not a rock symphony. I don't write that vulgar music. I only write serious music for intellectual people. Listen to this. I've just written it.'

'You've just written it? You've only been sitting there for three minutes.'

'We geniuses do things like that.' Percy twiddled some knobs. 'Now listen to my new symphony.'

The room was filled with discordant noises so loud that they made Weasely cover his ears and cling to a chair for support. He didn't know anything about classical music, but if it was the same as rock, then Percy had just discovered another great hit – it was certainly loud and discordant enough, even without the amplification.

Weasely saw Percy speak on the phone, and soon a thin, hungry-looking music student, with a violin under his arm, arrived at the garage and, although Weasely couldn't hear what was being said, he saw Percy hand over a very large sum of money, and then saw the student sitting down and writing pages and pages of squiggles which, even Weasely knew, were called notes.

During this period, Percy's personality underwent a complete change. He had tied his long, unkempt hair back into a very neat but artistic ponytail, had changed quickly into good clothes and, with that noise still pouring out of the machine, picked up a pencil and began to conduct the cacophony. His face was serious, indeed grave, and he nodded and looked to the left and right of his orchestra, and from time to time pointed his baton at a particular instrument. The effect was grand. When the music finished, at last, Weasely felt compelled to clap and to shout – as he'd seen on the telly – 'Bravo, bravo, bravo!' Percy bowed graciously to the huge, imaginary crowd, smiling condescendingly, while the student kept writing and writing and writing, for some hours into the night.

While they were waiting for the notes to be written, Percy contacted his agent, told him to engage the Opera House for a one and only performance of the new seminal work of the twenty-first century – the new atonal, existential, phenomenology-inspired work of the composer Percival Playbackavakoff. It was to be called *The Silent Scream for Canon and Kalnishnocov.*

The symphony was duly performed and went on tour. It was acclaimed by critics throughout the world as the work of the age. The current leading dumb blonde movie actress – who was tone deaf and completely illiterate – declared, during a photo shoot, in which she was totally naked except for a bunch of grapes, that the symphony was a work of genius, so, of course, everyone agreed instantly. Percy cashed in on this with interviews, his own photo shoots, and personal appearances. Gifts poured in, including a Lamborghini, a penthouse suite, a grand piano, and clothes galore from all the best shops – and, most importantly, plenty of the moolah.

Percy became famous for his humility; indeed, he was very proud of it. He spoke simply and quietly at functions in his honour, never claimed to be anything special, and spoke quietly, with solemn dignity, of his God-given gift. He also spoke touchingly of his manager and financial advisor, Mr W. Led.

Everything in the garden was going well when the music student wrote his blackmail note. Percy delegated him to Weasely – he seemed to be the expert in what Percy liked to call the Removals Department. With the music student gone, all would have continued well had not one precocious twelve-year-old brat in the audience – who had been reading the *Emperor's New Clothes* – possessed the weird gift of hearing things backwards. It was he who jumped up in the middle of a recital of the symphony – held before a crowd of seven thousand adoring fans – and shouted, 'We've been conned. It's just the *1812 Overture* played backwards.'

The orchestra stopped in dismay, and everyone looked for the conductor. Strangely enough, he was nowhere to be seen.

*

Later that evening, Weasely helped Percy stand on a kitchen chair and personally tied the knot in the rope. He didn't bother waiting for Percy to kick away the chair; he kicked it away himself.

Two months later, in Argentina, leaning back in a cane lounge and sipping a cool drink, Mr Weasely Led sighed as he thought briefly of the late Percy Playback. Well, it was a good trick while it lasted, but nothing lasts forever. He lifted his glass to his now departed friend, and once again congratulated himself on his own shrewd practice. He'd made sure the bank accounts were all in his name, and he chose Argentina as it didn't have an extradition policy. He could now relax in peace, and never have to listen to any music at all, rock or pseudo classical! Life had now become pure bliss.

The Long and the Short of It

The Crown Prosecutor, Lionel Long, adjusted his thick reading spectacles, peered briefly at his typed page, tugged at his barrister's wig, composed his face and turned to make his final address to the jury. 'Ladies and gentlemen of the jury, this is a sad day for our country, for all those values we hold most dear – the values we learned at our mothers' knees – and, indeed, it's a sad day for the whole of society in general.

'Today, you see before you a young man who had the whole world before him, not yet twenty-five years of age, a graduate from a well-known university, holding down a worthy position, and about to marry a fine young woman – the daughter of a church warden – and, as any decent person among us would think, one who would be looking forward to a happy and responsible law-abiding family life.

'And, what do we see, ladies and gentlemen? We now see, beneath the smooth, good-looking, clean-cut exterior, a seething mass of deceit. We see malice and, yes, downright evil. We see a mind capable of the most heinous crime of all – the crime of murder!

'And murder for what end, I hear you ask yourselves – and well you should. Was it to steal a huge cache of jewels? A fabulous emerald necklace? Perhaps bars of bullion? No, it was not! It was to steal the life savings of an old age pensioner, by the name of Mrs Amy Dogget, who lived alone in a bedsit with the use of a lavatory at the end of the corridor.

'Amy Doggett had been a widow for twenty-two years, and for all those long and weary years, she had struggled to supplement her tiny income by charring in the block of offices off the main Hampton Road. Each evening, Amy left her bedsit at six-fifteen p.m. and trudged along Hampton Road in her well-worn, but brilliantly polished, old shoes, to her gruelling hours of slavery.

'This dear, faithful old soul had one aim in life: to finish paying the debt for the huge white statue of an angel – with plaster draperies – that she had erected by the side of her husband Herbert's grave. The angel is a touching sight, ladies and gentlemen, its arm frozen in stately benediction, and Amy knew that Herbert slept soundly in the safe and sure hope of the resurrection, with his huge plaster angel guardian – very nearly paid for – beside him.

'Amy had managed to pay two hundred and seventy-two pounds, fifteen pence off the total price, but, despite all her efforts, there still remained sixty-three pounds and five pence left to pay. She had vowed, on her Herbert's grave, to finish the debt and, towards this end, saved every penny she could. She even went without food on many occasions, in order to fulfil her promise to her beloved husband of fifty years for whom she still grieved as though the death had been last Friday at noon as they shared a meagre fish finger luncheon and he had choked to death on a fish bone.

'Thus, each night at six-fifteen exactly, she set off for Hampton Road for her nightly drudgery, regardless of the weather. Rain or fine, Amy was utterly dependable and worked in spite of her terrible rheumatism, her aching back problems and her frostbitten fingers, and her employers all rightly agreed, on oath, that she was the most reliable of all the workers they had on their books. With fifty seven pounds now saved in a tin soapbox under her bed, Amy could see the end of the debt for the angel in sight. All was going well until disaster struck!

'Ladies and gentlemen of the jury, Amy Doggett was visited one night – without invitation – by that evil man you see standing in the dock! Well might you squirm and strive to run away, sir, you vile creature. Hold him tightly, officers! You'll not escape so easily as that. We know his sort, do we not, ladies and gentlemen of the jury? Let me now tell you the details of this creature's crime. I would prefer to say to you, shield your ears, but you must know these terrible and ghastly details in order to fulfil your duty as sworn members of this august panel of jurors.

'Not only did this monster of iniquity enter the chaste chamber of this elderly lady and rob this dear old soul of her pitiful savings – which I would like to call the angel's tribute – but he did not stop there! No, sir! He proceeded from that evil to the deepest level of depravity: he murdered her! A cruel and bloody murder!

'And what a murder! Was it committed in a way designed to spare the frail, old woman as much pain as possible? It was, in fact, exactly the opposite! It was committed to cause the greatest agony imaginable! Just put yourself in the old lady's place, ladies and gentlemen. Just imagine the terror of being nearly garrotted. You're gasping for breath. Each breath is a burning, painful sensation. Then you discover you're tied in such a way that the rope goes around your neck and is then tied to your bent knees, so that every unwary movement you make could result in your strangulation.

'If this were not enough, this unspeakable creature…this bounder… went further. To the strangling cord, he added four knife wounds – not one of the four fatal, in itself – but each causing great loss of blood, so that, eventually, if the victim didn't strangle herself, she would bleed to death, which is what poor Mrs Amy Doggett did. She bled to death all over her one and only precious possession, her new square of green and black check linoleum.

'The murderer entered the pensioner's bedsit by using a device, common to people of his profession and which most of us know as skeleton keys. This indicates that this was not a one-off job, a sudden yielding to the impulse of the moment, but a careful premeditated crime. This man was obviously a professional.

'How will his poor fiancée be able to face the world again once this news is noised around? The good woman – I believe her name is Hermione – is prostrate with grief at the moment, so I am told, and will most probably have to go abroad, in all probability, living in hiding for the rest of her days. And no wonder! The shame of being known to be attached to this caricature – who shares the appearance of a man but is, in reality, a beast from Hell!

'Let me tell you a secret, ladies and gentlemen, which will give you an indication of the character of this evil man. He gave me all the information about his fiancée in the hope that it would pull the wool over my eyes, that I would not see the deceit he was practising, not only on me, but on that poor defenceless little woman, Hermione, waiting at home, no doubt at the time of the crime, embroidering her gown, as she was preparing modestly for her holy nuptials.

'I have little more to say, ladies and gentlemen. You have heard the evidence, you know what this creature has done, you know the plight of that poor, old lady, Mrs Doggett – lying dead in a pool of her own blood on her green and black check linoleum, in the midst of her grinding poverty, and for what? For a few measly pounds! That's what! This creature of the devil, standing in the dock, murdered a dear, sweet little old lady for a few pounds!

'Ladies and gentlemen of the jury, I leave his fate in your hands. If you do not insist on the ultimate penalty, then be it on your own heads if you cannot sleep at night for fear of criminals such as he. They could well be coming after each one of you this very night!

'My lord, I rest my case.'

The judge spoke, 'Mr…er…er…Short. Would you like a brief recess, or do you wish to make your final speech for the defence to the jury now?'

The defence barrister, Mr Stephen Short, stood up. 'Now, thank you, my lord. It will not take long, not nearly as long as that of my learned colleague, Mr Lionel Long.

'In fact, my lord, and ladies and gentlemen of the jury, there is no defence needed at all. You see, my lord, the man standing in the dock is totally innocent, as he is the wrong man. The criminal escaped this morning from his cell. The man who is standing in the dock is Mr Brian Upton. He is an usher of this very court. He went to bring the prisoner to the courtroom, was overcome and found himself locked in, and the prisoner gone.' Mr Short sat down.

The man in the dock shouted in exasperation, 'That's what I've been trying to say for the last half hour, but that old windbag Mr Long – he's as blind as a bat – wouldn't shut up long enough for me to get a word out.'

The court was in uproar.

*

The laughter that this story evoked in all the inns of court reverberated throughout every known legal chambers in the city. The prosecutor, Mr Lionel Long, made an immediate appointment to have his cataracts removed – he had been putting it off for years. Afterwards, he had to take a long cruise to recover from his dreadful humiliation. It's an embarrassing episode, but to tell the truth, the whole truth and nothing but the truth, that's the long and the short of it!

Prometheus Hated Vultures…

Lady Agatha Thornthistle was a formidable woman. She seemed even taller than her six feet two inches. Her rather small head, with its beak-like nose resting on an elongated neck, was inclined to make her look a little like a bird of prey. This impression was not helped by her tendency to lean forward as she walked, and her predilection for wearing a long black cloak which flapped in the wind like huge wings.

The friends who knew Agatha intimately (and that was not a large number) knew that she had a romantic streak – hidden, of course – and within that unprepossessing exterior beat a heart that yearned to do wonderful and thrilling deeds. After a long study of ancient Greek history, she found what she had been looking for all her life: a Cause, a Mission – an opportunity to shine with the greats of the past. It was nothing less than the noble determination to free Prometheus.

She lay in bed at night, her mind in anguish, as she thought about his precarious position on the cliff face. She was also gravely concerned about his mental condition as well. Agatha had recently undergone surgery, and with her vivid imagination, she easily empathised with the poor victim of the gods' revenge. The very thought of having to face major surgery every single day – having his liver ripped out by a vulture – was almost too terrible to contemplate. She was uncertain whether it was a blessing, or a curse, that his liver regrew each night; it only meant that he had to endure the agony all over again each day.

And for what, Agatha asked angrily. Simply for stealing fire from the gods! They were a mean lot, and no mistake – the whole lot of them; always either fighting each other or devising cruel punishments to inflict on people. They kept the fire as they didn't intend to get cold in the winter; it didn't matter about the poor people freezing below. Prometheus had done a great service to mankind, and it was up to someone to rescue him. Agatha, the middle-aged, eccentric romantic, decided she was the person to do the deed.

Agatha made the decision calmly, and began to prepare a list of what she would need. First of all there was a vulture – that was essential – then special boots for climbing the cliff face, and finally, good, strong bolt-cutters. Where would she get those things? That was easy. Harrods of course! That store prided itself you could buy anything in the world you needed there – if you had the money. Agatha paused. Did she have that the right way round? Perhaps it was everything you never needed? Didn't matter; the store would surely have what she required.

Dressing hurriedly on a cold wintry day in February, clutching her list in her hand, she set off for Harrods.

*

Lady Agatha, her umbrella in her rather knobbly hand, advanced in a determined manner towards the sales person, her pince-nez clamped firmly in place.

'Miss,' Agatha demanded loudly.

The saleswoman turned round, pretending she hadn't seen the customer coming towards her, and summoned up a phoney smile of welcome. She had served this troublesome woman many times before. 'My Lady, how delightful to see you again! It's always a pleasure to serve you.'

'Nonsense! You know it isn't. You could at least begin by speaking the truth, miss, or is it that revolting Ms nonsense – sounds like a bee buzzing.'

The woman hesitated, unsure which answer to give. She decided to be brave, and face the consequences. 'It actually is Ms, ma'am. I've always been partial to bees.'

'Humph! Well that at least explains your peculiar choice of clothes.'

The woman was indignant. 'I beg your pardon!'

'Granted. Now listen carefully. I'm looking for a large vulture.'

'I beg your pardon?'

'I've already said it was granted. Are you in need of a hearing aid? Now about the vulture: I'll need a big one.'

'I'm confused, My Lady. A big what?'

'I suggest you do see a doctor. You obviously are hard of hearing. Is there anyone else who could serve me, preferably someone who isn't a Ms?'

The saleswoman turned in relief to a floor walker who was hastening towards her. He had seen her surreptitious signalling. The woman managed to whisper to the man, 'The old dame wants to buy a vulture,' and then turned back to Agatha. 'My Lady, I think Mr Bottomley is the right person to serve you. He most definitely is not a Ms.'

The man smiled and turned his suave charm on this eccentric woman, thinking he would quietly lead her to the restaurant, where they would give her a cup of tea and send her on her way – you always had a few loonies among the aristocracy.

Unfortunately, Mr Bottomley took Agatha by the arm and tried to guide her in the right direction. Agatha was furious. She pulled herself away from the man and, armed with her umbrella, which now was shown to have a long sharp metal ferrule at its end, threatened to run him through if he did not remove his hand from her person.

A small crowd began to gather, and a loud-mouthed, vulgar young man shouted, 'Good on you, Granny! Sock it to him, the snooty bugger.'

Several youngsters in the crowd cheered.

Mr Bottomley tried another tack. He apologised profusely for his mistake, and asked Agatha if she would just tell him what she wanted, he would see that she got it; he would stake his reputation on it.

Agatha lowered her umbrella. 'Take me to your bird department immediately. I'll select the bird myself.'

Mr Bottomley looked relieved. It was now clear the old dear simply wanted to buy a sweet little bird, perhaps a canary or a budgerigar. He smiled patronisingly and assured Agatha she would find all she needed in their splendid aviary department and would be delighted with the chap who managed the department. His name was Mr Simon Sparrow.

Simon Sparrow was a tiny man, thin and balding. He had a tendency to hop from one foot to the other. Although he lived his life in the midst of pretty little birds of all shapes and colours, he longed, as did Agatha, for adventure – heroic if possible – with cliff-hanging excitement; a life that rose beyond the confines of caged canaries whose twittering matched the inane conversation of the clientele.

Simon listened enthralled as Agatha made her demands for a vulture, and was even more entranced when she actually informed him of her plans to free Prometheus. Here was adventure indeed! Agatha, for her part, in response to Simon's enthusiastic reception of her demands and her agenda, expanded and blossomed at this unusual attention and interest – people usually yawned politely when she held forth. Within the space of ten minutes, they were chatting away like two old friends. Almost without realising what she was doing, Agatha suddenly asked the little man to come as her companion and assist her in this adventure. To her astonishment and delight, Simon Sparrow knelt on the carpeted floor of the store at her feet.

'My Lady! You have been sent by the very gods themselves! Nothing would be more delightful. And,' he paused for a quick breath, 'I can arrange for us to collect the vulture when we arrive in Greece. That way, we can avoid any difficulties in getting it through customs here.' He stood up and dusted his knees. 'Oh! There are a dozen things to arrange before we can set off. Would you take tea in the restaurant while I give notice and collect what's owing to me?'

Agatha smiled at the little man and did as was suggested, reminding him that he must remember she was footing all the bills incurred in the adventure, including of course all the equipment he would need. Simon actually gasped in his gratitude, and both he and the lady went off in their respective directions.

Three hours later, their purchases complete and their air travel arranged, they left the store and arranged to meet the next day at the airport. Agatha was so excited that her adventure was actually about to begin, she had great difficulty in sleeping, so it was long before the sun had even thought of rising that she was up and dressed, wearing her riding breeches and climbing boots, and arrived at the airport hours earlier than she was expected. But, lo and behold, there was Simon already there, in his little shorts and big boots; he looked like a little boy dressed up in his father's sports clothes. However, his eyes were shining with excitement and, seeing Agatha, he rushed forward and clasped her hand and kept hold of it for the whole journey. Agatha, surprisingly, obviously didn't mind this familiarity; she made no attempt to free her hand.

It was a pleasant flight, and the two new friends chatted easily and made plans for the rescue. They would collect the bird and make their way immediately to Mount Olympus. There, they would make camp and prepare for the rigours of the next day by digging into a hamper Agatha had brought with her from Fortnum and Masons. She thoroughly believed in the health-giving properties of pâté and caviar. If one was going to rough it, then one might as well do it in style, was her motto. She had also included a bottle of champagne in case of emergencies – and, as everyone knows, thirst is an emergency.

They collected the vulture and were surprised to find that the price had been reduced. The owner of the shop explained that the bird was depressed; it was missing its companion and was off its feed. Its huge wings drooped despondently, but thankfully, it took to little Simon immediately. Once the shop owner had fixed up the shoulder pad, the bird sat contentedly on Simon's shoulder, which made him actually taller than Agatha. The bird rubbed its terrible beak lovingly against the thin hair of his head, but apart from giving him a gravel rash, there was no harm done. Simon realised that it was done through affection, not with evil intent, and patted his new friend lovingly.

The intrepid couple had a little difficulty with the driver, who recoiled in horror when they tried to enter the coach with a vulture. However, a hefty bribe by Agatha reconciled him to his fate. But, just to make sure, he dashed off to get his rifle, which he kept by his side the whole of the journey.

Arriving at their destination, Simon set up camp in a professional manner – he had been a boy cub (he had never graduated to boy scout)

– and soon they were happily eating their way through the hamper and giving choice pieces to their new friend who they discovered, from a name tag, was female and was named Penelope. The bird seemed to realise she was among friends, and settled down without a murmur. Simon, just to be on the safe side, kept the little collar on the bird, and the lightweight, but very strong, chain was attached to his wrist. However, it allowed Penelope to move around fifty yards or so, and then fly back to Simon's shoulder; her weight, when landing, sent him crashing to the ground each time, but he soon became used to it.

As soon as night fell, Penelope folded her head under her wings and began to snore softly. Simon lowered himself to the ground gently, so as not to wake the bird, and both he and Penelope slept soundly unaware that the very air about them was filled with Harpies, Furies and Dryads. Even Narcissus, sitting close by the water's edge, and muttering cries of amazement at his own beauty, failed to spoil his slumber. Agatha, as was proper, had retired modestly to the tent, full of food and bubbly, a bit inclined to hiccup but at peace with the world.

The big day broke brilliantly clear with the promise of great heat to come. After breakfast, the adventurers donned the rest of their climbing gear and, with Penelope perched on Simon's shoulder, began preparations for the perilous climb to the ledge where poor Prometheus was preparing to face yet another bout of major surgery.

It seemed the cliff stretched upwards right to the sky, and for a few moments, both Simon's and Agatha's spirits faulted. They were apprehensive; they feared they would never be able to climb this terrifying rock wall! It was Simon who overcame his fear first and then encouraged his new, and rapidly becoming very dear, companion. The woman felt a little more reassured when Simon explained to her that she would be tied to him round the waist at all times, so even if she did slip and lose her footing, he would be holding her safely. This was remarkable encouragement from a small man who had never climbed higher than the second step of a ladder in his life, but it did the trick. Agatha's spirits were now renewed, and she then reminded Simon of the rescue plan.

When they had climbed high enough to see Prometheus, the moment he saw the surgeon vulture Asklepios, he was to release Penelope, who would immediately attack the vicious bird, as he was now in her territory – Agatha had been assured this is what would happen; they would then cut the prisoner loose with the bolt-cutters she wore at her waist. After all was done, they would then make the decision to either climb upwards, or downwards, depending on which was closer. They would thus have saved the heroic young man from his terrible fate.

Simon nodded his acceptance of the plan and now, really excited, both rescuers raced towards the cliff face, forgetting that Simon had Penelope on his shoulder. Agatha soon had a firm grip on the wall of rock, but disaster struck quickly. Penelope, seeing a rock wall in front of her, did the only thing sensible for her to do: she unfurled her great wings and rose spectacularly into the air. And it was spectacular indeed. She had, in the blink of an eye, lifted Simon fifty yards in the air, and he was turning somersaults at an alarming rate at the end of the bird's chain. But not just Simon! Poor Agatha, pulled from the wall face, was dangling upside down, helpless, tied to Simon's waist and gasping for breath.

As soon as she looked up, she saw the surgeon vulture approaching, and yelled to Simon, 'Cut Penelope loose, Simon. Asklepios is here! Quickly now!'

Simon, now completely disoriented, heard the shouting and, as he tried to get at his little knife, the new vulture, uttering strange and terrifying noises, was making straight for him. He screamed, a thin streak of sound in the racket made by the birds' wings, but then saw to his amazement that the vulture was dancing in the air around Penelope, who was making similar sounds of happiness; at long last, the two vultures had each found their long lost partner. They were deliriously happy.

In their joy, the two birds flew aerobatics around each other, swooping under and over, and up and down, until Simon had no idea where he was, except for the alarming fact that he was a very long way, indeed, from the ground, while poor Agatha was performing gymnastic feats of remarkable skills – for her age – a hundred feet below.

Agatha, in a brief moment of lucidity, when she saw which way was up, screamed to Simon again, 'Simon, cut Penelope loose or we're lost!'

Poor Simon did understand that, and taking his knife he made a hurried slash with it and accidentally cut Agatha loose, instead of the bird! As a result, he shot suddenly, at terrifying speed, up into the air, dangling from Penelope's chain, while Agatha began the horrific fall to her death so far below.

However, it was not to be. Agatha praying frantically as she fell, suddenly had her fall arrested; she fell into the strong, brawny, muscular arms of Prometheus standing on his ledge. He had watched the whole drama and realised that this intrepid woman had risked her life to try to save him. He looked at the figure in his arms and thought she was the most beautiful creature in the whole world – it is to be remembered he had been on the rock for a very long time and was a cousin of Oedipus the King – and fell in love with her instantly; madly and crazily in love.

Agatha, for her part, seeing the beautiful Adonis who had rescued her, forgot poor Simon instantly. She rose shakily to her feet and handed the handsome brute of a man the bolt-cutters. He quickly cut himself free then returned to his wooing of this lovely woman who had saved him from a life of intensive care recovery.

After a suitable period, they decided on their future. They would get married quickly by a Greek priest, who was good at abseiling, and then set up home in the cave behind the ledge. Agatha was thrilled and was soon busy making plans for some chintz for the curtains and the cave opening, a couple of comfortable easy chairs for taking the air of an evening and new furnishings inside as well. The busy couple, having the tourist trade in mind, decided to extend the rock ledge platform and fit in a barbecue. That would attract climbers and provide extra pocket money. They would be the happiest couple in the whole of Greece. Agatha thought her husband the most handsome of men and, in time, came to accept the very large scars across his tummy – they had been cut so expertly that they had healed beautifully.

Strange to say, they were never again troubled by the vulture Asklepios.

In fact, as Penelope had immediately recognised, it was not the doctor at all, but her long-awaited husband Ulysses, back from his adventures. Ulysses had only been moonlighting as the famous doctor as he had been suffering from a cash flow problem. Now, with his wife restored to him, he settled down with Penelope, and raised a big family which was a credit to the species. Penelope found, when she first returned to their nest, her loom – still there after all the years of separation from her true love. She was overcome with emotion and cradled the loom in her wings, while scaly tears fell from her eyes. She then hurled the hated machine from her; she would now be freed from that tedious weaving and unpicking in the long years she had waited for her erring husband to return.

Thus true love had solved the problems besetting Prometheus, the vultures and Agatha Thornthistle…but…

What about poor Simon?

*

It's a sad tale, but then this is ancient Greece and very few of the stories end happily.

Simon was taken by Penelope to Ulysses' nest high up on a mountain top and sat in the midst of the other chicks as the eggs hatched. He was not much bigger than they were. He was well looked after, never wanted for food, and they never treated him badly. In fact, he was always the favourite chick with his new mother, Penelope, but he knew he could never compete with the others in flying or in zooming down on their food, but Penelope taught him a new skill: he learned how to grasp the victim with his hands and carry it for her as she flew back to the nest. That was a great help for Penelope, especially as she grew older and her strength began to fail. He also began to win bungee-jumping competitions, and became quite famous; he had absolutely no fear of heights at all now.

Simon and Penelope remained close always, and he became reconciled to al fresco air travelling dangling from the mother bird. It was certainly cheaper to travel this way, and he saw more of the world than he had ever thought possible in his previous life. To tell the complete – and somewhat disturbing – truth, it did not take many years before, to his surprise, Simon, as his own hair began to go, discovered that feathers were starting to push their way through his scalp, and he began to flap his arms in a singular fashion.

Very strange, indeed…but then, remember, as you well know, it's all Greek to me!

A Bedtime Fairy Story

'Please, Bugs, it'll only take a few minutes,' Sandra Butts pleaded with her brother. 'I've got my hands full, as you can see. If Dave were home, he'd do it, but now he's inside, I've got all the kids to cope with myself.' She lifted the youngest infant onto her lap and began to attend to his feeding.

Now, Bugs was not what you would call fastidious, but there were certain things that he drew the line at, and this was one of them. He had spoken to his sister before about her attitude towards breastfeeding in public, and it had no effect. So, in order to avoid the embarrassing sight of his youngest nephew being fed, he hastily agreed to tell the rest of the brood a story before they went to sleep. He got up wearily from the sofa and followed the five little children up the stairs wondering what on earth he could possibly say to them.

Bugs knew that it was customary to tell fairy stories to little children. The problem was, with the sort of life he led, he knew little about such stories. He was certainly used to telling stories – especially to the police – but fairy stories? As he walked very slowly up the stairs, Bugs's mind ranged over three decades to the time when he was a nipper. He was trying desperately to remember a jumble of bits and pieces of stories his father had told him– that had been before the poor old chap was blown up in that bank job which went wrong.

He knew how they all began – the 'once upon a time' bit – but what came next? He also was pretty sure about the ending as well: 'And they all lived happily ever after.' What a load of bilge! However, he was stuck with it so he'd just do the best he could. He should have thought of this before he decided to pay his sister a short visit.

Bugs took so long to get up those stairs that when he arrived in the big room where all the children slept, they were all in bed and wearing that particularly innocent look of young children ready for sleep.

Bugs asked them what story they would like and they all wanted a different one. That was no good so he tried another dodge. 'I've decided,' he announced boldly, 'to tell you a brand new story that has never been told before.'

There were ecstatic cries of delight from the children. Bugs settled himself comfortably on the only chair in the room and, with his mind in a positive chaos of characters, plots, scenes and jumbled thoughts, began his story.

'Once upon a time…'

There were groans from the oldest child – a cynical child of seven.

Bugs frowned at him and the child subsided quickly; it didn't do to be too smart with Uncle Bugs – he had a solid right hand!

When total silence reigned once more, Bugs continued. 'There was a beautiful girl who had become a princess through accidentally kissing a frog and eating a green apple instead of the red one, and she lived on a high balcony and would never have been able to get down from there had she not let her hair grow ever so long. It grew so long that she was able to use it as a ladder to get to the ground. The landlord of the house was a wooden-faced man with a long nose which kept growing longer each time he told a lie.

'The beautiful princess lived along a yellow brick road where the only men around were made of tin or straw, except for young Rudolfus – a prince of the neighbouring city. Rudolfus was tall and strong, with wonderful long legs, but had an aunt who looked like a wolf and loved eating little girls dressed in red. He tried to talk his aunt out of this unhygienic habit, but to no avail.

'He decided on drastic action so took her to a special tea party where the queen herself was presiding. He tried to follow the queen's advice, but she was drunk and kept shouting, "Off with her head," which didn't go down very well with Aunty, so they hurried away and stayed a little while with Mary, who was worried about her little lamb, which was unwell.

'The aunt was a bit of a dab hand at natural medicines, so she uttered a spell and whipped up a dose of arsenic by crushing dozens of apple seeds together and mixed them with a little milk. She gave this to the lamb to drink. The aunt insisted, for some reason, that they leave Mary immediately and they both hurried away. Mary never did have any trouble with that lamb ever again.

'On their way home, they encountered Jack Sprat, who was crying in a corner with his thumb in his mouth. It appeared that he had eaten someone's pie and sold some magic beans for a cow and now everyone was laughing at him.

'The prince, who was a kind chap, thought he would help out, so suggested that Jack plant the cow – it might be magical as well. Jack threw the cow in a hole in the ground in a fit of pique and, lo and behold, from the ground up shot the biggest, fattest beanstalk you ever did see, which kept mooing. Jack went up the beanstalk as fast as he could, eating beans all the way. He had quite suddenly become a vegetarian and only ate greens. He was soon out of sight with a stomach disorder.

'As the prince was passing the ocean shore at the time, he waved to old King Cole, who was bathing in the waves with three fiddlers to keep him company. The king was ordering the waves to stop, and they refused to obey him. He then demanded that the Knave of Hearts immediately bring him the burnt dish of tarts to throw them into the water as a punishment. They were immediately eaten by a mermaid who screamed loudly to Jack and Jill to give her a drink – she had burnt her throat quite badly. Jack and Jill were busy, but a boy with an apple on his head with an arrow through it rushed to get the poor mermaid a drink, while his father, using another arrow, shot Humpty Dumpty, who fell into a pie, and four and twenty blackbirds rose screaming from the dish in a terrible fright.

'Mary Poppins was passing by, and the prince hailed her. She stopped in mid-flight – not at all pleased – and demanded to know what the prince wanted. He told her he was in love with the girl with the long golden hair who lived on a balcony and asked her advice what to do about it. Mary, understandably, was irritated and told the prince to go to the girl and tell her of his love, and to stop bothering her. She was on her way to see Jack in the hospital. The termites had gotten at the base of the beanstalk and he had had a terrible fall. He could not eat any fat from that time onwards – only his wife could. It was fortunate that he still had the golden egg clutched in his hand. His wife wore it as a lopsided earring.

'Unfortunately for the prince, he didn't know that the giant had fallen down as well as Jack. He had been to the balcony and kissed the girl with the golden hair, and she had immediately fallen asleep. The giant happily told the prince that the girl would sleep for a hundred years.

'The prince was undeterred. He declared that he would remain faithful and would wait for her, no matter how long it was. There was a big meeting of all the characters in all the stories, who tried their hardest to talk the prince out of his mad scheme, but no, he was adamant: he would wait for his beloved balcony girl.

'One hundred years later, the beautiful princess woke up and stretched luxuriantly. She looked in wonderment at the very, very, old man standing beside her bed. It was the prince. He was 122 years old, and looked older! He said, "My beloved, at last you are awake, now we can be together forever!"

'Now, kids, I'd like to say that they lived happily ever afterwards but that wouldn't be true. The beautiful princess took one look at her ancient lover and screamed, "Not on your life, you old lecherous lout. Get away or I'll call the cops."

'But everything was not lost. The giant suddenly turned up again looking not one day older – giants age very slowly – and he kissed the princess, now wide-awake, and she turned into a frog. The giant was delighted so, buying a large fish tank, he threw her in and dashed off up the beanstalk, which he had repaired during the long years he had been waiting. The princess, now a frog, croaked loudly, "Abide with me" and was never heard of again.

'The very old prince was very upset, as you can imagine, but just then another young prince came along and he was some sort of shoe salesman. However, as he only carried one shoe with him, business was obviously not too good. He kept trying to fit the shoe on to young ladies' feet. A sweet little old lady with white hair and rheumatics had left her precious shoe in the care of her horrible sisters and when the prince arrived at their house, the two sisters claimed the other shoe as theirs. They claimed the prince as well, so he had to marry both of them. The sweet little lady, who had been done out of her rightful husband, came weeping to her old friend – her very old friend – the old prince, and do you know what? They fell in love and decided to marry and stay together for the rest of their lives.

'The old prince and Cinders (that was the name of the old lady) were hurrying to the church, the prince in his wheelchair, when they came across Little Bo Peep who, having lost her flock, was picking the daisies that Jack was pushing up as he didn't survive the fall from the beanstalk all those years ago.

'The young girl was crying when she came across Frankenstein and they fell in love instantly. They married and in time produced seventeen little Frankensteins, all nuts and bolts and screws, but dear little chaps. Bo Peep had difficulty with the first little one as it did not thrive on milk, and all his screws became rusty. She consulted the owl as the wisest person in Beatrice Potter's books on Victorian cooking, and good old Beattie – her father was a bookie – told her to use oil, and all would be well. Bo Peep kept an oilcan near her and soon all the bolts and screws were glistening. It made cooking so much easier for little Bo with her large family.

'So, in the end, everybody – at least all the good people who went to sleep when they were told, otherwise they'd get a belt over their ears quick smart – lived happily ever afterwards.

'Now go to sleep, or I'll get on to the giant. I have his mobile and he'll deal with you. Goodnight.'

The children were very polite and waited until their uncle had left the room before they said what they really thought of his story. Believe it or not, although thrilled to have remembered all the stories correctly, Bugs was surprised to find he was never again asked to tell them a story.

The War of the Roses or Another Day at the Office

Cecily, duchess of York, wearing in her hair the compulsory white rose of her house, sat in her parlour really ploughing into a plate of bread and honey; she had missed breakfast because of a stupid argument with her husband's steward and was ravenous. She was always ready for the table and was the envy of her female friends – which was not a very large group – as she always stayed trim and attractive, although to be truthful, her breath was a little sour. However, if you used a fan, you could easily come quite close to her and not feel faint.

As Cecily munched away, she pondered the problem of her hated rival, Margaret of Anjou. It was bad enough when the woman's pathetic husband, Henry VI, was alive, but as a widow Margaret was definitely worse! The nerve of her to be pregnant! To be carrying his child! How dare she? No wonder, Cecily reasoned, Richard was so angry he refused to release his steward to let him take her precious Pou-Pou for his little walkies.

It had been that which had led to the disagreement Cecily endured in the marital chamber that morning with the insufferable steward – he obviously belonged to the other house. Come to think of it, he spent much of his spare time in the red rose garden. Taking another slab of bread and smothering it in honey, Cecily pondered the enigmatic steward. He looks Welsh as well as having a Welsh name, she thought, so he could well be from that blighted country, and everyone knew you couldn't trust that lot any farther than you could throw a javelin.

Cecily's mind wandered to another of her problems: her chambermaid. She gnashed her teeth, which wasn't as easy as it sounds, as her mouth was full of honey. What a load of hypocrisy, the steward pretending she was his daughter! 'Zounds!' she snorted. 'Tell that to the fairies! If she's his daughter, I'm the Queen of the May!'

The duchess clapped her hands angrily, and a hot towel was handed to her immediately. She cleansed her hands quickly and slid the towel carelessly across her mouth, leaving it shining with spilt honey. She was now in a hurry to see Richard to discuss the situation they were in, so stalked with long strides, her draperies floating behind her, to the duke's apartment. She was now determined; he must deal, once and for all, with the steward, Glen-dour-ffink (with two ffs) and his brazen paramour, Rougelll (with three llls) at once.

Richard, Duke of York, had been slumped in his chair reading when Cecily arrived at the door, but he stood with alacrity as his wife barged into his inner sanctum. He kissed her messily, which left him with honey all over his beard. He hastily tried to remove the worst of the damage while he ushered his heavily pregnant wife to the window seat in the castle wall.

'Sit, dear, and don't stress yourself,' he advised. 'Remember the hopes of the whole York clan rest on the child you are carrying. Do you think you're getting closer than you thought yesterday?'

'Don't be ridiculous, Richard,' Cecily snapped. 'The birth can't be altered just to suit our plans. Margaret may still give birth before me, God forbid, forsooth, and all that.' Cecily sat up straighter, adjusting her gown. 'Richard, forget the child for a moment. I want to talk to you about that vulgar strumpet of a chambermaid of mine, the...'

'The pretty, rose-red daughter of old Glen-dour-ffink? A nice girl, I thought...'

Cecily was outraged and interrupted loudly. 'Are you mad, sire? I have reason to believe that Three llls is in the pay of the enemy. She's no more the daughter of Two ffs than I am.' Cecily was aware that Richard wasn't listening; he'd gone back to reading a small book, under cover of the desk. She raised her voice and spoke icily. 'And so I killed the girl and pickled her in cider.'

She looked up to see the effect of her last statement, and was furious to hear her worst doubts confirmed, as Richard murmured inattentively, 'That's nice, dear. We could have it for supper.'

Cecily stamped her foot, and demanded in a loud voice, 'Richard, put down that book this instant, and tell me just what it is you are reading.'

Richard looked a little shamefaced. 'Dear, you know my page, Joyelin, has been experimenting with time travel?'

'Umm?'

'Well, he actually landed up this time in a funny place with a strange Italianate name called Ah-mer-ee-kah.' The duke started to laugh. 'Would you believe it, honey…that's what the men called the women in that place. Seems appropriate today – they claim that the year is 2001!'

Cecily sighed wearily. 'Really, Richard, sometimes I despair of you. When are you ever going to grow up? No child over the age of five would believe such nonsense! However, that does not explain the book. Is it about us? About our great families?' A sudden suspicion awoke in her breast; her formidable brows drew close together. 'It isn't a romance, is it, Richard?'

'I don't know what you would call it, Cecily, but it's really interesting reading. It's about an English king and queen, just like us, who have a fearful female enemy and they end up murdering the girl and shutting her in the window seat of a castle – just like the one you are sitting on, dear. It gave me ideas.' Richard's smile, as he said this, should have made her suspicious, but Cicely noticed nothing and went on to express her opinion of the book.

'How perfectly disgusting! They must be barbarians, if they existed at all.'

Richard was anxious to tell the rest of the story. 'Listen, dear, after the murder is done a – de-tect-tiff, I think that's what he's called – a sort of crowner, I expect – comes in and solves the mystery, proves the king did the killing. The king's taken away and the physicians bleed him to death by putting something into the vein in his arm.'

Cecily stood up. 'I've never heard anything so ridiculous in my life. As if there could be anyone lying here dead in the window seat…'

The duchess lifted the lid of the seat and shrieked wildly. Lying at her feet was the pretty Welsh girl with the three llls in her name. Stuck in the breast of the young girl was a beautiful red rose – as well as a nasty dagger.

Cecily staggered away from the seat, her finger pointing to the rose. 'Richard, what have you done? She's wearing the Lancastrian colours, a red rose...'

The door burst open and the steward hurled himself at the duke. 'Don't try to escape, you murdering monster!'

Richard clasped his breast in the tragic gesture of despair as he heard the accusation. 'Glen-dour-ffinch! Have you lost your wits?' he gasped.

'I'm not Two ffs at all. That was my disguise. I am the crowner, and I saw you stab the poor child, Three llls, just because she happened to be born on the right side of the blanket, but a Lancastrian blanket. She would be next in line to the throne after Margaret's infant.'

Richard made a dash for it, but it was too late. Guards rushed in, together with physicians, who began making unpleasant preparations, with knives and lancets.

The shock held Cecily rigid for a moment; she then rushed forward, only to be held firmly by the arms of a hefty woman wearing yet another red rose. A loyal servant got off one shot with his crossbow but it only took off the nose of Cecily's opponent, but the doughty woman only flinched, shook off the remnant of the nose, and held on even more tightly to the duchess.

Cecily was then taken from the room – the duchess hastily snitching, undetected, the novel Richard had been reading, as she walked past his desk – into the corridor, where she was then, to her complete surprise, set free. She went back to her parlour, where she was soon engrossed in Richard's strange book. She couldn't put it down; she had never read anything before in her life like it. My goodness, she thought, the monks who would have written it by hand must have been extraordinarily clever – either that, or were possessed by the devil. She had never seen handwriting like this. Cecily looked up as the cook brought in a large pie for testing by her grace. The duchess knew her priorities; she had the dinner to supervise, so interrupted her reading immediately to attend to the cook.

To give Cecily her due, she didn't carry on a treat over Richard's fate.

As she heard his final scream, then the gigantic splash, she knew he had either escaped by jumping from the window into the moat, or else he was dead, so she shrugged and dismissed him from her mind. Her thoughts were now back on the dinner, and so she plunged her knife into the pie. To her amazement, out flew twenty-four black birds, all carrying roses – some red, some white.

The cook cried, 'Gawd a'mercy, yer grease! It's a sign, mum, that be what 'tis!'

The duchess shouted. 'Count the number of whites and reds, Cookie!' and then, having delegated the job, went back to her reading.

As her mistress read, the cook was counting frantically. When she faced her mistress at last, her voice was trembling, 'Mum, t'were fourteen reds, but t'were only ten white roses.'

'Now don't take on, Cookie,' consoled Cecily, patting the faithful retainer on her plump arm, 'as this extraordinary Inspector McLaren says from Scotland Yard…'

Cook was aghast, and interrupted. 'He lives in a yard, mum? Must be awful draughty in that bleak, windy country!'

'That's as may be, Cook, but what he says is,' Cecily carefully adjusted the book so she could see it clearly. Finding the place, she read the line, shrugging philosophically, as she imagined the, no doubt very cold, very wet, inspector from Scotland would have done:

'You win some and you lose some,' Cecily sighed and closed the book. 'Ah well, tomorrow's another day. Now about dinner, Cook. We'll have the other pie, the one with veal in it.'

Hey Diddle Muddle

For the seventh day running, the following, foolish little nursery rhyme had been prominent on the front page of the *London Times*:

> Hey diddle diddle,
> The cat and the fiddle,
> The cow jumped over the moon.
> The little dog laughed to see such fun,
> And the dish ran away with the spoon.

'It's an outrage, Holmes-a'Cat,' declared Dr Watson-Meerkat, commonly known as 'Watty'. 'They're making fun of you.'

The great detective lay back in his easy chair, his arm hanging over the side, his fingers playing with the bow of his violin. 'Now, don't get too upset, Watty. We've had some tough cases before, and we'll manage this one as well. I think this could well be a three-pipe case.' Holmes-a'Cat paused, took up his bow, and now pointed it at Watson-Meerkat. 'It does have its interesting features, though. I mean, the whole mystery hinges on the fact that the dog did laugh. It did not remain silent.'

'Oh, come now, Holmes-a'Cat, old fellow. That's pretty obvious to me: the dog was amused when he saw the cow doing somersaults, that's all.'

'Really, Watty, you can be unbelievably obtuse at times. Believe me, when I can understand why the dog laughed, I shall have solved the case.' The detective picked up his violin. 'Now listen carefully, Watty. I think I've got the hang of this instrument now.'

Watty grimaced and gritted his teeth as his friend began to play. He hoped desperately that his friend would get past the beginner's pages, and get onto some decent music; or else give the wretched thing away and take up an instrument which was easier to play. To distract himself from the scraping of wrong notes and excruciating chords, Watson pondered the latest case that had been dumped, albeit reluctantly, into Holmes-a'Cat's lap. It had begun seven days ago when the first strange notice was seen in the newspaper.

The advertisement appeared after several strange happenings had taken place in rural England. These had been on such a scale that questions had been asked in the House, and the Minister for Agriculture had been inundated with furious demands from outraged farmers wanting to know just what he intended doing about it all. To make matters worse, milkmaids had gone on strike, declaring that they absolutely refused to go traipsing through space looking for the dratted cows; first it was the moon, but where would it all end? It just wasn't on; very rudely they had stated that London could whistle for its milk.

Scotland Yard had its best brains working on the problem but, so far, they had come up with nothing; they had no idea who was behind the whole scheme. After the Yard had admitted defeat, the government had been forced to place the whole affair in the hands of the private detective, Sherlick Holmes-a'Cat.

Watson-Meerkat was irritated with his friend. He thought they should be up and doing, not just sitting in their rooms in Baker Street, playing badly on the violin. Holmes-a'Cat was stubbornly indolent at times. With this case, he refused to stir, and announced, with a certainty that was bordering on smugness, that the problem would come to them, not they to it.

Watty thought he would have to buy earplugs if he had to listen to any more of the violin, so made a great deal of noise cleaning his pipe and clearing his throat. Happening to glance out the window, he saw something which he thought would do the trick to gain Holmes-a'Cat's attention.

'I say, Holmes-a'Cat, sorry to interrupt your splendid music, but a dashed pretty young female has just come along the footpath. I do believe she's heading in this direction.'

Holmes-a'Cat put down the violin quickly, and went to the window. 'Come here, Watty. I want to teach you something: listen and learn from me.'

Watty dutifully hurried to the window, where he had a better sight of the pretty youngster.

'You see that girl, Watty?' Holmes-a'Cat said. 'Let me tell you definitively, she is obviously from the country, possibly Dorset…'

'Holmes-a'Cat, don't be ridiculous. She has just this minute stepped off an omnibus from Stepney.'

Unperturbed, Holmes-a'Cat went on, 'You can see how unused she is to city streets. See how painfully she walks.'

'But that's because she is wearing ridiculously high heels.'

'Yes, she's also is a very religious girl, but very poor.'

'For heaven's sake, man, she's wearing expensive clothes of the latest cut, and is carrying a bag on which is written the words "Atheists Unite".'

'As I thought: a clergyman's daughter! I would say she conducts the choir in the church. See the little baton she is absent-mindedly chewing as she walks along?'

'This is beyond belief! Are you feeling all right, old chap? She's smoking a cigarette, for goodness' sake, from a long cigarette holder.'

Watty was prevented from saying more by a knock on the door, and Mrs Hudson – who, although Persian, spoke English – announced in a cold voice, with a tight smile, disapproval in her eyes, 'A person to see you, Mr Holmes-a'Cat. She says she's Miss Pussy Wildcat.' The landlady left the room abruptly, closing the door noisily to express her displeasure.

Holmes-a'Cat moved forward to meet the beautiful creature, when she stumbled and fell neatly into his arms. Miss Wildcat made no attempt to remove herself, nor did Holmes-a'Cat. It was left to Watson-Meerkat to drag the girl from Holmes and deposit her, none too gently, into an armchair.

Watty was having no more of her nonsense. 'Now, state your business, and be quick about it. You can then leave the way you came in. We have no time to waste on people like you – it's obvious what you are.'

The girl was furious. She leapt to her feet, dragged up her long skirt and extracted a small but deadly revolver from the top of her stocking. The two men stepped back.

'Now, you'll listen to me, both of you…' began the girl, then held up her hand. 'As you're both gentlemen, I ask you to let me have a moment, then we'll continue.' So saying, she laid down the revolver and tore off her very tight corset. 'My girdle was killing me,' she explained. 'And now for these wretched shoes. How can women walk in these idiotic things?' The shoes were also cast aside, and then came the greatest surprise of all: Miss Wildcat reached up her scarlet fingernails to her forehead, ripped off the very clever mask she was wearing and, standing before the two men, was an all too familiar, terrible figure.

'By Gad!' Watty gasped. 'Holmes-a'Cat, it's…'

'Professor Moggiarty,' concluded the great man. 'I've been expecting you.'

Moggiarty quickly picked up the revolver again. 'I thought you were when I read your little advertisement in the personal column of the *Daily Mail* this morning, saying you knew it all.'

Watty interrupted the conversation. He was still shaken; he thought he was seeing the ghost of the professor. 'How can you be here when you were drowned, with my esteemed friend, in the waters of the…'

'Richenbath Falls,' finished Moggiarty.

'Not Richenbath. Richenbach, Moggiarty,' corrected Holmes-a'Cat automatically.

'Don't be ridiculous,' objected Moggiarty. 'We both had a good bath, so the place is called Richenbath.'

Holmes-a'Cat sighed; it was useless arguing with this stupid man.

The professor turned on his old enemy. 'So how, my highly renowned, completely incompetent and illiterate musician, can you say that you know everything? Even my dog laughed at that.'

Holmes-a'Cat shouted in triumph. '*Now* I do! From your own lips you have revealed the solution to the clue that eluded me: the question about the dog. The dog belonged to you! That's why it laughed.'

'Of course, but what about the cows leaping into space?'

'They never left the ground. You've been up to your old tricks again with hashish, haven't you? You had those poor foolish girls stoned out of their minds. I'm right, aren't I?'

'Curse you! You are! But how can you explain the dish and the spoon?'

'That's easy. For the past month, I have been reading in the personal columns your passionate messages to your sweetheart – the poor foolish girl. She's the girl who advertises spoons in the advertisements in the paper. She's called the Spoon Girl. You called yourself a super dish of a fellow, swept the girl off her feet and abducted her, and she's now locked up in your castle in Transylvania, where she's pining for her real true love: poor pimply-faced Tom who works in the fish market – she always was a pushover for fish.' The great detective paused, and then added, 'Watty and I will go and rescue her, after we've dealt with you.'

Moggiarty laughed a nasty sinister laugh. 'And just how will you accomplish that? I have the revolver, you might remember. Oh! Stop it. That hurt, you beast!'

While he had been talking, Watty had drawn his swordstick and quickly and efficiently struck the wrist of the professor, causing the revolver to skid harmlessly across the floor, where Holmes-a'Cat picked it up and examined it leisurely.

The tables were now turned, which gave the room a much more pleasant outlook, and while the professor stood helpless before them, he asked piteously, 'How did you recognise me? What I suffered in that outfit, you wouldn't believe.'

'It was your whiskers,' calmly explained Holmes-a'Cat. 'While we were struggling in the waters of the falls, I noticed that your whiskers moved in a unique manner. I made a note of it at the time and determined to write a monograph on it when I had more time.'

Moggiarty was heard to mutter, 'Those dratted whiskers, they've betrayed me again.'

Watty, ever practical, asked, 'Well, Holmes-a'Cat, what are we going to do with this fellow?'

'Why, what a strange question, Watty! Hand him over to Scotland Yard of course. They're waiting in the next room. Inspector Lestrange is in Thailand, so, when I cabled to him yesterday for assistance, he sent a couple of Siamese police to assist me.'

After the police had left the building with a swearing Moggiarty, trussed up like an eel ready for the pot, Holmes-a'Cat looked at his friend and smiled. 'Sorry, old fellow. I couldn't resist kidding you with all that nonsense about the girl. I knew it was the professor as soon as I saw the whiskers.' He picked up his violin and asked happily. 'Now, we've finished yet another case, Watty, let's celebrate with a concerto for violin. I know you'll enjoy that.'

Watty looked desperate. His brain working furiously he stumbled on an idea. 'Holmes-a'Cat, you know that nothing could please me more, but I think we should consider you, not me. You deserve a feast: a feast of the most delicious seafood – a feast to set before a king. Let's go to the Golden Herring and enjoy a wonderful dinner. I know I'm hungry, and you must be starving – you always are, at the completion of a case.'

Before the great man could reply, Watty had rushed from the room, shouting over his shoulder, 'Get yourself smartly set up, old man – wear your topper – while I whistle for a cab.'

Within a few minutes they were driving at breakneck speed down Baker Street in a hansom cab. Holmes-a'Cat was holding on tightly, while Watson-Meerkat was silently giving thanks that he had avoided another boring night listening to that wretched violin.

*

And that's how Hey Diddle Muddle turned into a Hey Diddle Fiddle and then, once solved, became again Hey Diddle Diddle. Once again, as so many times before, Holmes – even if he were now a cat – from his rooms in Baker Street – had saved the reputation and honour of England.

Jack the Dipper

Jack Casey was genuinely proud of his trade. After all, he had learned it at his mother's knee. In her day, Molly Casey had been one of the best pickpockets the city had ever known. She had only been caught twice, and spent an uncomfortable number of months each time in what she loved to call 'durance vile'. However, even there, she made use of her time and honed her skills to such perfection that the very warders guarding her discovered they were continually losing handkerchiefs, lipsticks, keys and other small items. They usually found them fairly quickly by raiding Molly's cell.

Just as with any other good mother, Molly was anxious to pass on to her only son all she had learned, and to share the values and skills she herself treasured most highly. That was how it came about that Jack, from his earliest years at school, learned to use his hands in a way that was unusual – to say the very least – compared with other boys his age.

One of the most important lessons Jack learned was to try always to protect his hands from possible damage. For this reason he couldn't play football, cricket or tennis at school for fear of damaging the 'precious tools of his trade'. This didn't make him many friends at school but, with his mother's encouragement, Jack realised if he wanted to reach his life's ambition to be the best pickpocket in the trade, he just had to put up with being a bit unpopular.

During the evenings, Molly and Jack practised and practised the various methods and routines of their work. There was the 'careless boy bumping into the prosperous man or woman routine' – while the fingers slid inside the coat or into the purse. When this was perfected, Molly taught the 'shy, embarrassed young child routine' – the one where the boy accidentally bumps into a person and holds on to them to save himself falling, while uttering endless, endearing apologies. This went down well, especially as Jack looked so innocent, even angelic, as a child – and even as a young adult.

As Jack's fingers grew long and slender, he did hours of exercise with them to make them very strong, but still very thin and flexible. He kept his nails longer than most males – they were useful as a type of pincer instrument, particularly for extracting objects from trouser pockets. The 'hip pocket routine' Jack found the hardest, especially if people were wearing jeans. The jeans were usually so tight that they formed a natural seal for the back pocket, which was a real problem, as that was the place where the wallets usually were.

To overcome this problem, Molly had Jack resort to the old 'razor blade trick': perfecting the slitting of the base of the back pocket in one quick swipe, grabbing the wallet as it fell through the hole, then disappearing into the crowd of shoppers.

But this trick did not come easily. Night after night, Jack practised on Molly, dressed in skin-tight jeans. Many a night there were real screams of anguish from Molly as Jack misjudged the slash. But, in time, both mother and son were satisfied he had finally got the hang of it. Molly was particularly relieved when this part of the course was over; the wounds healed fairly quickly.

From the age of twelve, Jack was working the crowds. He had about six methods of attack, and was so successful that it was a very rare day that he did not collect a great deal. Molly went with Jack to the various crowded venues and shopping malls. She sat herself down in one of the easy benches usually provided for the public, often fanning herself to pretend she was exhausted, while clutching a big, open leather bag in her left hand. From time to time, Jack would suddenly appear next to her on the seat, never speaking, and stay a moment near her, neatly dropping his takings into the open bag. When there were credit cards, Molly used them immediately – if they were usable – in various stores to buy the things she needed, or what Jack had asked her to buy for him. She then discarded them so that they could be found by other people.

It was quite an exhausting day's work. By the time evening had come, both mother and son were glad to be heading home carrying their hot take-away dinner with them. After dinner at home, they would spend a couple of hours counting the daily proceeds and planning the next venture. They had to travel a lot, rarely going back to the same place within the space of twelve months.

During the next five years, Molly and Jack did extremely well. The police were mystified at the rise in the crime statistics. The poor police were constantly being abused by the press, the shops, the mall-owners and by the individuals who had been the victims of these clever pickpockets. Some of the senior police thought there must be a new gang operating.

But one young police constable, Detective Constable Barbara Heavythwaite, had other ideas. Barbara was twenty-eight, weighed seventeen stone, and was determined to catch the ones responsible for the crimes herself. She realised that these crimes all followed the same pattern; she had worked out the six methods from the recorded interviews of the victims, and sought among the records for any previous similarities.

She came across the record of a Molly Casey and was immediately interested. Doing more research, she found that Molly had a son. Barbara began to wonder if he had followed in his mother's footsteps – perhaps they even worked together. When Barbara was finally able to discover the present whereabouts of Molly, she was staggered to see that two people drawing welfare cheques could live in a house that was a veritable mansion and drive a Ferrari. The constable found that there was also an apartment in Monte Carlo in Molly's name as well! By this time, Barbara decided her search was over – she had found the culprits!

Next day, the young detective constable, suitably disguised in a shocking-pink jogging outfit – which made her look like a young elephant with bad dress sense – followed Molly and Jack to the mall, where they began to work. Barbara let her large handbag fall open, revealing her purse and several notes as well. Jack saw the windfall and, in a well-rehearsed move, his hand flashed into the bag. To his bewilderment, the same hand was suddenly being held in a vice-like grip by fingers of steel – he was trapped! He attempted to squirm out of the police officer's grasp but it was to no avail. Barbara's seventeen stone left him helpless.

'Take me back to your mother, Jack,' she ordered, and keeping her fingers firmly locked around Jack's wrist, was soon standing in front of Molly who, looking up, realised that the worst had happened. Now they were both in for it! She tried to console herself by reflecting that Jack, as a first offender, would get off lightly but she also realised that, as an old lag, she would cop it badly.

The constable's words cut through her thoughts. 'It's time we had a good talk, Molly,' Constable Heavythwaite stated. 'Just get up naturally and lead the way to the car park. You will drive your own car home and Jack will be with me in my car. Don't try to be clever. Jack will be handcuffed to the dashboard of my car. When we get to your house, just go in as usual and open the garage door for us – we'll be right behind you.'

'But, I don't understand…' began Molly.

'You will. Now move!'

Jack was totally bewildered. Of course he had acknowledged the possibility that he could be nabbed one day, but he thought he would be taken to the police station, not back home. He let himself be handcuffed to the bar on the dashboard, as Barbara heaved her bulk into the car and drove to their home. They were soon seated around the kitchen table, a cup of tea before each of them. Molly sat next to Jack and together they looked with apprehension at this unusual police officer.

'Now, you two,' began Barbara, 'I've decided on a new plan. You, Molly,' the officer pointed a fat finger at the older woman, 'will be retiring to Monaco. You'll leave tomorrow. You will not be returning. As the house is in Jack's name, he and I will keep it. He will marry me by special licence, and I shall take your place in your very lucrative scheme.'

Jack was startled. He had nothing against marriage itself; many of his friends were married. But he had thought that when the time came, he would have at least a say in the matter. He started to protest, but Barbara cut him short.

'Enough of that, my lad,' she warned. 'If you don't agree to the new arrangements, then I shall see you get at least ten years in the pen. I'll add a few extra charges to the list, including the attempted rape…'

'The *what*?' Jack shouted.

'You heard me. You're a young strong man and I'm a helpless female…'

'Helpless!' Jack muttered. He turned to his mother.

To his surprise, she was smiling at him. 'Jack, it won't be too bad. I've wanted to retire for some time now, and I shall love being in Monaco. I was worried about you not having a partner and now here you have one. It's a good idea, officer, to get married: you can't give evidence against each other then.'

'As I'm about to become a member of the family, Molly, you'd better call me Barbara, not officer. I shall be resigning from the force tomorrow, to concentrate on our new career.' She leaned forward, and leering at Jack, patted his hand. 'It's going to be great fun, isn't it, Jack?'

The young man cowered back in his chair and actually shuddered. Married to this female hippopotamus would be a fate worse than death. Something had to be done and done quickly – done now! He couldn't risk this woman leaving the house. He had to act while this obese policewoman was still here in their house and at their mercy.

In an instant, Jack ceased being a youth and became a man. He leapt for the carving knife, and in the twinkling of an eye had sliced Barbara down the middle. He was deaf to Molly's cries to protect the new linoleum. Jack finished his work, took all the credit cards they had collected that day, together with stacks of cash, and stashed them in the constable's pockets. He then ordered his mother to help him carry the great weight of the obese woman out to the police car – thoughtfully parked inside their own garage – then drove away with the body. After leaving the car and corpse in the sleaziest part of the city, he walked all the way home. Once there, he burnt all his clothes in the furnace and then showered three times. He was delighted to see that Molly had scrubbed the floor of the kitchen clean. The new linoleum was gleaming.

Before he went to bed – it had been an exhausting day – he rang the airline and booked two seats on the early flight to France. It would do him good, he decided, to have a holiday with Molly. Perhaps they would stay on a bit for the season; there was no hurry to get back.

Safely sitting in the sun in Monaco one week later, Jack read aloud to this mother a snippet from the English paper he had bought. It concerned a female police officer, Detective Constable Barbara Heavythwaite, who was found posthumously guilty of all the crimes he and his mother had committed. The police claimed that, as the evidence was found on the body of the dead woman, it was obvious she had been killed by a rival gang. They apologised to the public on behalf of their colleague and promised a full enquiry. Molly, righteously indignant, declared it was outrageous – and Jack agreed with her – that things had come to a pretty pass when you couldn't trust even the police of today!

There was a strange sequel to this event. Jack, who had taken pride in calling himself the Dip, or Jack the Dipper, discovered he had accidentally found his real calling in the slicing of Barbara. He had really enjoyed that, and so he had a career change, becoming known, in time, as Jack the Ripper.

The rest is history.

The Sad But True Secret of Florian Fey

Florian Fey was a beautiful young woman. She had that ethereal quality that poets write about in breathless verse, yet was an approachable, and well liked, member of her little village community. Her parents had been killed in an accident when Florian was eleven, and she had lived through a sad, and often lonely, period in her young life, but, at twenty, she had blossomed into a warm and loving woman, liked equally by men and women.

When her studies were completed, Florian returned to her old home and began to restore the old mansion in which she had grown up, as well as the grounds. She worked hard and employed many tradesmen and groundsmen, until, eventually, the old place, on the edge of the village as it was, became something of a showplace to the local community; they were very proud of it.

The young woman had attended sales throughout the county collecting beautiful antique furniture and furnishings. Besides working on her beautiful house, Florian herself was involved in just about every village activity and was on all the committees. Her advice was always sought when difficult questions that concerned protocol or questions of taste were asked. She was regarded as a model of prudence, discretion and refinement. For this reason, when it happened, it was all the more remarkable and, indeed, shocking.

Late one Sunday morning, after returning from church, Florian, with tears in her eyes, hastily picked a small posy of flowers from her garden, and hurried to the small cottage of Mr Billy Bacon, the butcher. She knocked softly at the door. It was opened by a stout woman wearing an apron, who stared in astonishment at Florian with her gift of flowers.

'What on earth…' Mrs Bacon began, when Florian interrupted.

'I'm so sorry, Mrs Bacon, to hear of your husband's death…' She got no further.

The woman let out a shout. 'Are you mad, Miss Florian?' she demanded. 'My Billy is just finishing a large roast dinner, and he's drinking a pint of lager. What do you mean, his death?' The woman suddenly halted as she heard a scream from inside the house, so, dropping the flowers, she fled inside.

Florian was embarrassed and confused, so hurried away. She had not gone far when she heard the butcher's wife screaming. Florian, looking over her shoulder, saw her running out into the roadway to her neighbours to get help; she had found her husband dead at the table.

Of course, people talked. When Florian turned up at the church for the funeral, several people moved away from her in the seat; they looked at her with fear in their eyes. Florian flushed and kept her eyes down during the service.

If it had ended there, it would have all died down; people would have put it down to one of those strange coincidences that you find in life, but unfortunately, something occurred in the same week that sent shivers down the spines of the villagers.

Walking down the centre of the village main street one day, Florian was truly delighted to see young Jenny Walker taking her brand-new twins for their first outing in the pram. It was mid-morning and all the villagers were ready to admire and say sweet things about the beautiful young babies. They loved the young mother, Jenny and her husband Bert; both parents had been born and bred in the village, so everyone was anxious to see their first-born children.

There was an admiring crowd around the pram when Florian reached it. She and Jenny hugged; they had been at school together years ago. Florian was genuinely delighted to see the babies and looked closely at them, saying all the things that women do on such occasions, when she suddenly stopped short. She peered closely at the male twin, and her face grew troubled and sad. People noticed, and a deadly silence suddenly descended on the group.

'What is it, Florian?' asked Jenny, fearfully. 'What's wrong?'

Florian raised her sad face, her eyes actually filling with tears. 'Oh, I'm so sorry, Jenny. I wish it wasn't so, but the boy will not live longer than next Tuesday.' She then fled, running along the street towards her home, the tears flowing freely.

By the Monday night next, the baby boy was dead.

This time, there was no attempt to pass it over as just a coincidence. Something had to be done, but what? There was talk of getting the vicar to exorcise the woman, but he wasn't keen: Florian was one of his best workers in the parish.

While they were whispering in corners about the 'witchlike' behaviour of the young woman, another occurrence startled them nearly out of their wits.

It was at a meeting held in the village hall to discuss the preparations for the annual fete in aid of the church restoration programme. Florian, as a prominent – and generous – member of the committee, was seated on the platform.

The discussions had been going on for some time when the undertaker, Mr Burrows, stood up and spoke at quite unnecessary length of the mess made last year with the coconut shy confusion. Everyone grew restless, hoping he'd just shut up and sit down; all that was over and done with. Florian was seen to stare suddenly at Mr Burrows intently, and then stood up, her action so abrupt that the speaker was silenced with surprise.

It was then that Florian spoke coldly, without emotion. 'Mr Burrows, we have endured your harangue for fifteen minutes. You could have said what you needed in three. Why are you wasting our time, and your time, here when you should be at home to prevent your wife from running off with your assistant, Mr Spadefull, who, at this very moment, is leaving with your wife in his car. The car will crash tonight on the Benson bend. Both your wife and Mr Spadefull will be killed.'

Florian then seemed to stagger, and slowly fainted onto the floor of the rostrum, while the people ran from the hall in fright. The man and woman mentioned were killed exactly where Florian had said they would.

From that night onwards, no one ventured near Florian's house; the gardeners, the maids and the housekeeper all left. Florian was left entirely alone in that big, lonely, isolated mansion. The villagers crossed the road rather than walk past her house. A superstitious fear hung over the entire village, and poor Florian, struggling to keep the huge place going, had to do her shopping in a hole in the corner manner. If she entered a village store, the other customers left instantly. The doctor refused to come to her, and the dentist, seeing her coming up the stairs, hurriedly scribbled a note, and stuck it on his door: 'Gone on indefinite holiday'. This could not continue, so Florian herself decided to call a meeting of the entire village for the next evening.

The hall was filled when Florian entered and went to the stage. She stood there, a beautiful, lonely, pathetic creature, yet all hardened their hearts against the young woman; they were not having a witch living in their village if they could help it. Florian hoped, desperately, she could clear up the misunderstanding. She had to try to convince the people she was not a witch – if she couldn't, it really wasn't worth living there any more.

The meeting started reasonably well. The people listened as Florian reminded them she had lived there all her life with them, and they had always been her closest friends. She couldn't understand why they had done this to her; it wasn't her fault, in any way; she didn't ask to be different! Everything would have been fine had she stopped right there. Unfortunately she stopped dead in the middle of a sentence, and fixed the fire brigade chief with her penetrating eyes.

'Mr Blazer, I'm surprised to see you here tonight. Shouldn't you at least try to prevent your youngest daughter committing suicide just because she's pregnant to that worthless chap sitting next to you, Joe Balogna? No, it's too late now. She has just hung herself from the rafter in your barn. Oh well, as I was saying...' Florian stopped again and looked closely at the vicar.

The people held their breath – surely the vicar was safe? Apparently not!

The remorseless voice went on, 'Vicar, these good people deserve better of you. How dare you embezzle the funds raised to fix the church roof? You spent it gambling, and not in any respectable way – such as the horses – but on the dogs. How could you? It's so vulgar. However, you won't get away with it. The bishop has already been notified, and you will be moved from this parish tomorrow morning. And as for the vicar's wife, Mrs Gentrified, she's no more entitled to her endlessly repeated relationship to the Earl of Westminster than I am. She's a fraud – a good match for her fraudulent husband. They'll both be gone tomorrow. Mrs Longbarrow, I see you have your eldest son with you. Mike and I have always been friends. I hope he won't mind me telling you that he was the leader of the group that beat up poor old Mrs McGready, and robbed her of all her savings. However, the other gang members will stab you tonight, Mike, at ten thirty-three. Oh, there you are, little Mary Starling… I'm sorry, Mrs Starling, but Mary…'

Florian got not further.

Mrs Starling leapt to her feet, shouting, 'Stop her! Stop her! She's evil; that's what she is! Take back your curse on my one and only child, Mary, or I'll kill you myself.'

There was a rush towards the stage and it was only the united help of some men, under the poor vicar's directions, that got Florian off the stage and safely back to her own house.

Florian, once home again, came to herself with a start. What had she said and what had she done this time? No! It had to stop right now! The poor, tormented, young woman went outside and took a large hammer from the toolbox. She then went into a room that was always kept locked. Inside the room there was only one thing: a large mirror.

Florian took the hammer and struck three heavy blows at the mirror smashing it completely, but not before she heard her own voice saying from one glass piece, 'You will die tomorrow night. Go to the undertaker tomorrow morning and arrange your funeral.' The wretched voice then had the effrontery to add, 'It's been nice knowing you!'

'The nerve of her!' Florian muttered.

*

The next morning, Florian went to the undertaker's, and the tiny man, Mr Simperer (who had been hired after the unfortunate incident with the previous assistant) was surprised to find Miss Fey with her requirements all arranged: the coffin chosen, the details all written out; he was then given a cheque for the entire amount. The only question asked of him was a special favour: that Florian be permitted to lie in the coffin all that day. She assured the little man that she would cause no problems whatsoever, and would be gone by evening. He gave permission, inwardly thinking the woman was crazy, but with the cheque in his hot little hand, who was he to quibble at the eccentricities of wealthy people? He left her, thinking an hour at the most would see her out of the coffin, but he was wrong. When he was locking up that night, he glanced over at the coffin, saw Florian still there and, going to investigate, found her quite dead.

Florian left a strange will. She left everything – her house, all her possessions, even her jewellery – to the village church fund, to replace what the vicar had embezzled, but there was one strange codicil to the will. It warned the villagers against ever, ever, buying second-hand mirrors at a bring and buy sale. It was too dangerous: you never knew what could happen, or who could be in them.

Pandemonium in Paradise

Prelude

The Centurion: *Domine non sum dignus…* (Lord, I am not worthy…)
John the Baptist: *Ecce agnus Dei…* (Behold the Lamb of God…)

*

Flavius Antonius, the centurion – universally known and revered in heaven by the name Non-sum – was slightly put out when he received a message from Michael, the Great One, to see him immediately.

It wasn't that Non-sum didn't like Michael – as one warrior to another, he revered him. It was just that he was extremely busy with a new batch of recruits who were not shaping up well at all. Of all the groups of angels he had trained so far, he thought this lot would definitely need a lot of extra work before they were fit to be let loose on the world below, and he did so want to finish the morning's work… However…

Non-sum was used to taking orders, so, only pausing for a moment, he, with a well-practised twitch of his shoulders, put his wings neatly in line down his back. He didn't want to keep Michael waiting. He knew it must be important; Michael didn't waste time with trivial things.

He turned to his second in command. 'Look, Rufus, I've got to get up there to Michael. Put these gawky characters in pairs, and do non-stop sword training until I come back. Try to get it into their thick heads that they'll be engaged in battles! They're going to be fighters. They don't seem to realise that. This crowd need something more to motivate them than I've been able to give them. They think it's all going to be a breeze; I think they've seen too many of those pretty holy cards. Try to get it into

114

their thick heads they're going to face scheming and well-prepared enemy legions, so they must be highly trained fighters, or their opponents will eat them alive. After the sword training, take them to the gym for a few hours – it might help the puny little runts.'

Rufus began to look anxious.

'Now, don't worry, lad, just do the best you can. We can only work with the material they send us.' He clapped the younger man on the back and hurried to the main mansion.

As Non-sum entered the huge portal of Michael's headquarters, he noted the crowd waiting in the antechamber for the archangel. He felt embarrassed, as usual, when the secretaries – as soon as they saw the gold on his sleeves, and the final golden tip of his wing feathers – rushed to him and ushered him straight into the Presence. He knew it was a great honour but, even after all this time, he was still conscience of embarrassment and believed he was not worthy of so must deference. He was comforted by the thought that his friend, John the Baptist, felt awkward too, and for exactly the same reason. Well, that was easy to understand; neither of them had dreamed what would happen to the words they had once spoken, did they?

The Great Archangel Michael greeted his old friend warmly with a Roman hand clasp – which Non-sum had taught him. Michael was looking his age. As a veteran of so many campaigns, he was a little battered, but no more than one would expect of such a valiant warrior.

His office was dreadfully untidy, with books everywhere, mainly ledgers; papers falling from tables, and at least fifteen different CCTV screens that he monitored continually. It was a heavy responsibility he carried.

As he sat down, Non-sum studied his friend closely, noting the wilted wing feathers, and the tear in his tunic which still hadn't been mended.

Michael finished the paper he was signing, and pushing a button sent all the screens black. He then turned to Non-sum and smiled. 'A difficult one, Non-sum,' he began. 'A little skinny kid – about six or seven, Peter thinks.' Michael then leaned over closer to his friend and whispered.

'Between you and me, Non-sum, Peter's eyes are not too good these days. Well, it's understandable, of course, at his age.' Michael sat up straight again. 'I tell you that, as I don't know if the facts are exactly as Peter reported. He stated that this young kid was surprisingly obese as he was coming in the gate, and hurried away as quickly as he could. Peter thinks there's something suspicious going on. The kid could definitely be hiding something – Peter thought it might possibly be a bomb – and wants another earthling to have a look into it. He's from Egypt – the kid, that is, not the bomb. It could be from anywhere.'

'Oh, dear, and so I'm the earthling,' sighed Non-sum. 'Oh, well, I'll get on to it straight away.' He looked closely at his warrior friend. 'Don't get me wrong, Michael. I'm only too glad to be able to do something for dear old Peter. The only reason I sighed, I was anxious to get back to that new bunch of trainees I was sent.'

'What are they really like, Non-sum?'

'To be perfectly honest, Michael, not too crash hot. I've certainly had better.'

'I thought as much when I caught a quick glimpse of them passing by. You'd think they were off to a funfair. Have you managed to get them to stop wearing their haloes at a rakish angle? I couldn't believe my eyes. I thought they looked half drunk and I knew that couldn't be possible – this is a drink-free zone. However, their appearance is slovenly. I've never been able to put up with sloppy-looking soldiers.' Michael looked closely at his friend. 'Listen, Non-sum, don't knock yourself out over them. Try your best, and if they're really hopeless, toss them out. We'd be better off without them.'

'Well, they're still pretty raw, I'm sorry to say. I've left Rufus to try and get them to hone up on their swordplay, using the short sword. They'll probably succeed in harming each other most dreadfully – might do them good. I've never seen a wimpier lot. They'll need a lot of work.' He looked at the tired senior archangel, and softened his complaint; this poor chap had enough to deal with. 'Now, don't you be worrying, Michael. We've had some right clowns before this, but they've turned out to be valiant fighters and valuable guards in the end. I'll just have to work harder at this lot.' He stood up.

The archangel clasped his arm again in parting and, with a few instructions as to where to find the problem boy – who could just happen to be a terrorist – Non-sum left the office. Michael pressed the button which activated the screens, and was soon engrossed – back at work again.

Non-sum consulted his clipboard and saw that the name of the child was Ishak. As he walked to the small building where the boy was, he was revising what he knew of the situation in Egypt. It seemed fairly fluid. No wonder the little fellow was here; many children had arrived from there recently, and no wonder with all the bombing and fighting going on.

Arriving at the door of the single room, Non-sum heard a great scuffling as he called out the name and received no answer. However, when he announced that he was coming in, there appeared in the doorway a little child who seemed to be a strange mixture of shapes – he had bulges everywhere where he shouldn't have on his skinny body. What on earth was the matter with the child? Non-sum was about to grab hold of the boy and shake him to get rid of whatever he was hiding, when he happened to notice a long tail sticking out from under the hem of the boy's long tunic.

He smiled, and spoke gently to the child. 'Ishak, you can let the dog out now. You can't hide him any more – his tail is showing.'

The boy looked down and, seeing the tail, tears sprang up in his eyes. Trying to hide his tears, he raised his arms to his face, and the dog fell out from under the tunic.

The boy immediately knelt by the side of his dog, and began to plead with the stranger. 'Please, mister, please, don't take Lion away. I promise I'll look after him. No one will ever know he's here.' Ishak had his arms around the neck of the dog, which kept licking his face, while keeping one wary eye on the centurion.

'But, he can't stay here, you know that...'

A burst of crying interrupted Non-sum. 'He saved my life. Well, he tried to save my life,' hiccupped the child.

'Now, how did he do that?'

'When the bombing started, I was frightened and ran away, but with all the stones falling and the dust, I couldn't see where I was. I ran the wrong way and lost my parents and all my family. I ran straight into the middle of the fighting, where bullets were flying everywhere. I fell down and Lion lay right on top of me covering me.' The boy started to cry louder, and his grip on the dog grew tighter. 'They shot Lion. I heard him whimpering in pain above me, but he wouldn't move so they shot him six more times and only then did some of the bullets come through to me.' Ishak hiccupped. 'When my dad saw what Lion had done for me, he made them bury the two of us together. Please don't take him away.' The cries grew louder and louder.

Non-sum went to pick the boy up in his arms, but Lion, fearing the worst, bared his teeth, and set himself firmly in front of Ishak.

'First things first, my lad,' advised Non-sum. 'Tell Lion I'm a friend, and that all the people here are your friends. You needn't ever be afraid again, both of you, ever, ever. I promise you that.'

The boy looked searchingly at the tall Roman soldier, nodded, and then spoke seriously to his dog. Lion moved aside, and Non-sum picked up the child and held him in his brawny arms. Lion, aware now that his master was with friends, jumped up wagging his tail madly, and licked the stranger's arm.

Non-sum looked into the innocent eyes of the little boy, and then sat on the ground, perplexed, with the child on his lap. 'Now what on earth am I going to do with you two?' He looked at Ishak. 'Do you know your prayers, Ishak?' he asked.

'Indeed, I do,' replied the child and moving aside, knelt, with the dog beside him, and immediately began saying the Lord's Prayer in Arabic. As he prayed, something very strange and wonderful happened. The seven wounds on Lion's back suddenly shone out like precious stones – they were ruby red and glowing. The centurion moved quickly until he was kneeling besides the boy. Ishak, who, seeing the shining red gems gleaming on Lion's body, began praying again loudly, his head raised towards the

Holy One. The dog turned in the same direction and, putting his two front paws together, bowed his head to the ground.

The three of them were kneeling there on the ground in profound reverence, for a considerable time, then Non-sum arose and signalled to both boy and dog to listen to him closely. 'Now, let's consider this problem seriously, Ishak.'

Both of Non-sum's listeners paid close attention to his words.

'The trouble is, Ishak, you see, Lion is not christened.'

'Yes, sir, I do understand that,' replied Ishak. 'That's why I've been trying to christen him since I arrived here. I thought I'd keep him hidden until them. But,' his voice faltered, 'the strangest thing is, the water turns into beautiful, shining crystals as soon as it comes out of the jug. It never touches Lion's head.'

'That's because it's not meant to christen animal…I mean…personal pets.'

'Not even a martyr pet?' queried the boy tearfully.

'Well, as far as I know, not even for them.' He saw the boy close to tears again and said. 'Look, I'm no expert, and the Holy One has clearly indicated Lion has won favour with the Most High, so, possibly, just possibly, something could be arranged.'

Ishak took the man's hand and held it tight in gratitude, but the centurion shook his head warningly. 'Now, don't be getting your hopes up, lad. I'm not promising anything, I don't have that kind of authority.' He stood up. 'Well, I have a platoon of recruits waiting for me, so you'll have to come with me until I finish with them, and then we'll sort out your problem. Come on, Lion, you come too.'

Non-sum took the hand of the boy, and led the child and the dog back to the training ground for the recruits. Without thinking, he walked through the main assembly plaza, as it was the shortest way, but he was totally unaware of the attention he was getting. Everyone – every man and woman – stood stock still, staring at the dog in shock. As soon as they had passed, each person rushed off to their computers. Soon messages and demands were flying everywhere; officials were rushing to and fro, unsure what to do. Angels had to take to the air – there wasn't enough space on the ground; there were several collisions and, strangely for heaven, a great deal of noise. However, very soon – in fact, it was within an earthly heartbeat – the air was positively reverberating with the sound of animal noises. It was as if everyone had turned on their woofers at the same time.

Dogs by the million, cats in even greater numbers, monkeys, birds in cages and uncaged, talking parrots, white mice, some tigers, a rhinoceros and even an elephant soon filled the plaza to overflowing. Lions stood magnificently tall with their ruffs rampant, while a lone unicorn tried to be inconspicuous among a herd of zebras. The elephant was so excited he was causing havoc with his great trunk and his enormous feet, while his mahout, who had raised him from an infant, tried desperately to curb his excitement.

The elephant swung his long trunk from side to side unaware that he was knocking everything and everybody who stood in the way into the air. The five wise virgins went flying through the air at one stage and had to be rushed by angelic paramedics to the clinic run by the Archangel Raphael. Joseph, being a carpenter, was in great demand as so many buildings were damaged. He began organising all the tradesmen into groups to try to cope with the disaster. Being a practical man, and with so much experience, he soon had the workmen hard at work in the midst of the chaos surrounding them.

Some of the women, rescuing their pets, were trying desperately to keep them safe from other animals; they were also wondering just where they were going to buy cat and dog food – that is, if their pets still ate at all.

Martha, who hadn't changed very much at all, came charging out of her house, her apron flying, and declared loudly, 'If they think I'm cooking for this lot, they can think again.' She then caught sight of a giraffe and, frightened, ran screaming back inside her house.

The giraffe, unperturbed, gazed with curiosity into the upper windows of the buildings he passed causing nervous householders to scream loudly.

When the monkeys started swinging happily from every passing angel's foot, everyone thought that old Noah must have brought his wretched boat with him and the door had somehow been left open. Little Therese, always trying to pour oil on troubled waters, expressed the opinion that it was probably due to woodworm – the ark being so old now. Several of the older Carmelites smiled at this pretty thought, then looked at each other, shook their heads and raised their eyebrows knowingly.

Non-sum was blithely unaware of the havoc he had caused. He entered the stadium and closed the door on the rest of heaven. Rufus was very relieved to see him; he couldn't think of anything else for the recruits to do. The sword practice was finished, and the time in the gym was just about up.

Non-sum quickly called the recruits to order. 'That's enough. Stop gym work now and get in line.' He waited until they were standing in a group. In his parade ground voice, he shouted, 'Stand up straight! Number off, quickly now. Louder! Louder, I said, you wimpy creatures! Measure off! Straighten your haloes immediately – I'll deal personally with each one who disobeys an order.'

There was a frantic rush to obey, and haloes were quickly adjusted correctly.

'Now, you see I'm not alone. I've brought a child with me to show you something. I want you to see, at first hand, what you'll have to face and what you could suffer protecting your charges, by telling you a true story.'

Non-sum then repeated the story of Lion's magnificent attempt to save the boy's life. When he finished the details of the story, he added, 'And if you're wondering if that's what pleases the Holy One, let me show you something. If you work hard, every moment of your training, and then spend a lifetime of work with your charge, then, maybe, just maybe, you'll get a reward like this.'

Non-sum told Ishak to make Lion stand up with his back to the recruits and with his front legs on the boy's shoulders. He did so and the angels recoiled, first in horror at what had been done to the boy, and then, seeing the glory of the dog' wounds, turned reverently in the direction of the Holy One and bowed to the ground in adoration for the wonders of the miracle.

After this demonstration, the recruits – for the very first time – actually asked if the sword training could continue, and when this was granted, there was no slacking; each angel worked furiously exerting all his skill.

When Non-sum called a break, he was happy with the result. The sight of the boy and his dog had done the trick; the recruits were no longer fooling about. He and Rufus were smiling widely, and winked at each other. They were going to do it again; they were going to bring the whole group up to the required standard – the boy had done it!

Non-sum sat on the ground with Ishak and the dog, happy and at peace. It was all going to turn out well, after all his worry. He remembered Michael and thought he had better give him a call to let him know he had attended to both matters. He was just about to push the button of his cell phone attached to his left wing, when Michael's big voice came roaring through the phone.

'Non-sum, what have you done? We've got animals everywhere…'

'I don't understand. What do you mean?'

'Not only has Antony of Egypt got his pig and cockerel, but Paul of the Desert has the two lions that buried him, while Anthony of Padua has a whole menagerie – doves, lambs, cattle, you name it. And then one of the Desert Fathers has brought his crocodile! Can you believe it? A real crocodile! And then there's the elephant…'

'The elephant?' queried Non-sum weakly.

'Yes, a full-size elephant,' Michael shouted loudly. 'Remember the holy mahout who was martyred? He was saved the worst of the suffering by his elephant which was killed as well…' Michael made an exasperated noise. 'Oh, the noise, you wouldn't believe the noise!'

'Yes, I do believe it. I can hear it from here. The trumpeting of the elephant is so strong. But, Michael, I have an even bigger problem. I have to tell you about the Egyptian boy. I think your problem is related to him. Listen…' Non-sum quickly told Michael Ishak's story.

Michael was dumbfounded, and when Non-sum asked what he should do, he replied, 'Do? I have no idea what you should do. I've no idea what I should do either. We'll have to get a ruling on this…but shining like rubies, you say?'

'Yes, definitely rubies, very beautiful really, and he's a wonderful dog.'

'Um…yes, I dare say…but… Hold on.' Michael lowered his voice, 'I've got to go, Non-sum. Some of the Fathers have arrived. I'll leave the line open so you can hear the discussion.'

There were many voices speaking in the background, and then Michael whispered, 'Non-sum, Peter has just arrived and has asked for the boy and the dog to be brought to the meeting. Would you arrange that? Thank you – talk to you later.'

Non-sum sent the boy and the dog with one of his recruits and sat listening attentively to Michael as he called the meeting to order, but before he could speak, Augustine's authoritative voice came through loud and strong. He was using a loud hailer, speaking to an immense crowd. 'No, no! Listen to me! It's not what you think. I tell you again, no! The Parousia has not arrived. Quieten down everyone. The lion may be lying down with the lamb, but it seems as though it's only a practice run. As that's the case, for the time being, it's up to their owners to stop their pets from eating each another.'

Augustine put down the hailer, and turned to the assembled group of venerable ancients. 'Now, as regards the boy's request, I'm against it. The boy is fine, but animals are definitely not to be admitted. They all have to be put out.'

Cyril of Alexandria demurred. 'But, Augustine, this boy's dog has been marked out as special by the Holy One… I think…'

He was interrupted by Peter Chrysostom. 'Perhaps we could make an exception to the rule, brothers…perhaps christening?'

'Are you serious?' quickly interposed Iranaeus hotly. 'The only thing that could possibly be considered would be Baptism of Desire, and there are no grounds for that. I think if I remember rightly, Ambrose suggested…'

Mark interrupted quickly. 'No, that would never do, no matter who suggested it. Let me remind you of the last chapter of my Gospel. Our Holy Saviour said…'

'Yes, yes,' soothed Antony of Egypt quickly, anxious to avoid the uproar which would occur from the others if Mark started quoting from his own writings. 'I'm certainly all for letting the animals stay – everyone knows how fond I am of my pig – but let's forget the christening part. I was thinking more of a special reserve – a place set apart.'

'That is an interesting suggestion,' Justin Martyr said. 'I found in the University of Alexandria, and Catherine did also, that often it was possible to come to a solution to a problem through adopting another angle of thought…'

'I've never been interested in compromises, or angles of thought,' Origen cut in rather rudely. 'The situation is crystal clear. However, I must admit a reserve just might solve the problem. But, where, for goodness' sake?'

'It'll have to be somewhere close, otherwise there's no use in having the pets here at all,' Paul of the desert added sensibly. 'I think we should get the women's view on this.'

'You are a sensible chap, Paul – I think it must be all those dates you ate in the desert,' agreed Cyprian. 'Let's ask Catherine for her opinion.'

There was the sound of great movement, a rustle of skirts, and a little later the listener heard a female voice. 'I know the perfect place,' Catherine announced. 'I took some young people there for a seminar on Logic, not long ago. It's that spare cloud 22A. It's well stocked with plenty of water, handy for visits by owners, a little forest – that would be good for the monkeys – and far enough away for the noise not to worry anyone. The place is filled with plenty of flowers, so it's pretty as well.'

'The very place, Catherine,' declared Thomas of Acquin, smiling at the learned woman. He then turned to the whole group. 'I've been there. It's all that Professor Catherine said it is. I spent a time, and half a time, there revising the Summa.'

Peter had sat in on the meeting, listening but saying nothing. He now cleared his throat. The group immediately were silent, and looked expectantly at the elderly, venerable man.

'My sister and brothers, let me speak for a moment.' Peter had taken the boy on his lap, and the dog lay contentedly at his feet. 'For a long time now, I have had trouble trying to keep going on the gate. With all the wars and revolutions, it's been a very busy time there – especially with all the children. I was thinking of asking for retirement but I wonder if there is another way. Do you think that, with a little helper for the children – such as Ishak here – he, and Lion, could be the ones to welcome the children and be their guides? That would remove a great amount of work from me and I might be able to continue.' Peter smiled gently, 'I don't really want to retire at all, you know. I like my position there – despite all the jokes they make on earth about me at the gate.' He chuckled happily.

The meeting unanimously agreed that it was a splendid idea. There would then be only one single animal in heaven itself, and he would be actually involved in doing an important job for Peter. That couldn't be against the rules. The meeting also agreed that the other animals should all be transferred immediately to Cloud 22A – their owners could go with them and help them to settle in. There then followed a rash of details to be worked out regarding transport and so on. There were several opinions on every subject, as you would expect.

Peter listened and smiled gently. Ishak buried his head in the old man's chest and began to laugh with sheer happiness, and Lion, understanding that all was well again, licked Peter's sandalled feet. As the talking continued, Peter quietly slipped away, and soon man, boy and dog, were comfortably sitting before a little fire in Peter's lodge at the gates, toasting marshmallows.

In two times and a half a time, Ishak joyfully welcomed members of his own family to Paradise, and both he and his dog only left the lodge rarely, but they did go to the graduation ceremony of Non-sum's recruits, who all graduated summa cum laude. Non-sum and Rufus were very proud of their graduands and were looking very glamorous themselves in their very best Roman uniforms, all shining and sparkling.

The boy and dog served Peter faithfully and are still there, working and waiting to welcome people to their real and eternal home. Lion, in the midst of all the children, has never been happier. On cold, still, winter nights, if you really listen very hard, a person on earth can sometimes hear – as from a very long way off – a muffled bark, as boy and dog play happily together.

Zuppy Love

There never was a tale of greater woe
Than that of Zuppy and his hated foe!

I can't remember a time when I have never adored my master, Bertram St Clare. I suppose I must have had affection for my natural mother but, to tell the truth, I can hardly remember her at all.

I do remember my brothers and sisters, though – a thoroughly bad lot, in my opinion, always hogging the food supply, and snapping and nipping me just because I had the habit of being first at every meal. Of course, I do understand it was not easy for my mother – there being fourteen of us at the same time. I've no doubt my mother did the best she could, but she was only canine after all – she couldn't do the impossible. So, without any doubt, it was a relief when I heard that I was going to be given to a young boy of fourteen who was desperate to have a young dog that would be his very own. Apparently the boy's father – who must have been a horrible man as well as mentally afflicted – had hated dogs and refused to permit Bertram to have a dog up to this time. But Fortune smiled upon Bertram: his father fell under a train coming home from work one day. Thus, the way was suddenly clear for my master to fulfil his greatest desire – and of all the puppies to choose from, he chose *me*!

From the very first, we were inseparable – I think it was love at first sight for both of us. It was Bertram who gave me the name of Zuppy. I didn't care for it much, but my master chose it; that was enough for me. He was everything I have ever wanted in a master, and I tried my hardest from the very beginning to do everything he wanted, in exactly the way that he wanted it done. He had only to express the slightest displeasure at something I had done, and I never ever did it again.

When my master was not in prison – that's what I called the school he attended – he and I were together for every minute. Why he had to go to prison every morning is beyond me; I know he didn't want to go – he kept putting it off until it was almost too late for him to catch his bus. He kept running back to say goodbye to me, petting me and even kissing me on my forehead. I cried every morning when he went to prison, and counted the hours until he came back home to me again in the late afternoon.

That was the best time of all! My master hurriedly took off his special clothes and put on his old familiar ones – I was always happy when I sniffed those clothes – and he and I played and played and played. We had so many happy games, and nose-twitching walks as well. Oh, we did have such fun together!

Even at dinner time, although I had my meal earlier in the kitchen, my master allowed me to sit near his chair in the dining room and, from time to time, slipped me tasty morsels from his own plate. He did this secretly, and I was careful to be as secretive as he was – I did not want him to get into trouble because of me.

As Bertram grew older, he had more adventurous games. He bought a skateboard and taught me to skate on it. To be truthful, I didn't really like it at all and was always frightened I'd fall off, but Bertram was so proud of me being able to do it that I pretended I liked it, and wagged my tail happily when he hugged me after a successful long run on the board.

Bertram was also a scholar; he had a great love of English literature, especially the Bard. He loved to recite, by heart, the long wonderful soliloquies. I learned to love Shakespeare as well, and soon was able to quote large sections from the most famous of the speeches. Of course, I spoke Dog and others in the house couldn't understand me, but Bertram did. The others said, when I began 'To be or not to be…' that I was just whining, snorting and giving short barks, but Bertram said, 'No, he's repeating the speech I've just made. He's a very intelligent dog.' I felt so proud and practised during the day so that I'd be word-perfect for Bertram when he came back each afternoon from prison.

At night, right from the beginning, Bertram let me sleep in his room on the mat next to his bed. Let me tell you a secret: on very cold wintry nights, when there was frost in the air, Bertram whistled softly and I leapt up on his bed and he covered me with the doona. Often at night when I woke, I could hear his gentle breathing and I knew that everything in the world was all right: he and I were together and nothing was ever going to separate us – ever, ever, ever! As Robert Browning wrote, 'God was in His heavens and there, bones abound.' I think that was what the poet wrote – it sounds wrong somehow… Never mind, I must get on with my story.

Bertram was nearly twenty when a terrible thing happened in our lives. Her name was Felina – can you believe it? Felina! She said she was Thai but, as soon as I got a good sniff, I knew what she was! A designing hussy I could tell, right from the start! The bristles started to rise on my spine, and I growled deep in my throat. Bertram looked at me in amazement. I stared back at him, equally amazed. How could he even like anyone called by that hateful name is beyond me. But, tragically, Bertram not only liked the name, he fell in love with the horrible person who had the name. I just couldn't believe it.

Of course, I'll not deny Felina was beautiful – if you happen to like that type, but I did notice the shadow on her upper lip. Well, my lady, I thought, it won't be too long before you'll be needing electrolysis.

I did all the things I possibly could to warn my master. Every time Felina came into the room, I snarled and bared my teeth and growled menacingly. She only laughed and made things worse by making Bertram angry with me. Once when I had given her the tiniest little nip on the heel, to let her know just how much I hated her, my beloved master actually gave me a hard slap. I could hardly believe it! After all we had been to each other during all those years. I slunk away under one of the chairs and hid my eyes under my paws. My aching heart equalled that of Hamlet as he contemplated the bare bodkin, or that of Romeo waiting fruitlessly beneath the balcony for his Juliet.

After some time meditating on death – suicide in particular – I suddenly remembered a problem Cook was having in the kitchen with rats! My thoughts turned from suicide to…murder! Cook had put down arsenic – in the form of small olive-shaped pellets – to kill the rats and had warned me to be careful of the baits; they would kill me, she said, if I accidentally ate them.

I sat up straight and thought: here is a way out of this situation! Bertram will be free of her and we will be together again, just the two of us. Now how would I do it? I pondered this and an idea came to me. I knew she liked to have a cocktail when she arrived and Bertram usually had them ready for her – and he always placed an olive in her drink! I heard my master say that she was coming round at four o'clock, so I determined to put my plan into action.

Going to the kitchen, I carefully lifted the arsenic 'olive' in my front teeth being careful not to breathe in while I carried it into the sitting room. Bertram had the drinks already poured – with an olive in hers – on the table, and had gone to the door to let in the wretched creature. So, putting the poison down on the floor, I quickly removed the good olive from her drink, then took a very big breath, and held it as I lifted the poison to her glass, by putting my paws on a chair; I then dropped it in the drink. It was only then I could breathe again normally – which was a relief – I'm not good at holding my breath. I rushed outside and sluiced my mouth clean in the ornamental golden carp pond, then hurried back to see the result of my efforts.

She arrived and immediately went to the arms of my master. This usually made me angry, but I was too nervous this time to take offence. After kissing Bertram, she went straight to her drink – she always had it in a pink glass; what else would you expect with a person with a name like Felina? Without pausing a minute, she drank off the poisoned drink and began chewing on the olive. Suddenly there was a lot of choking, glasses crashing, shouting and general mayhem. I added to the panic by barking very loudly and frightening everybody; I usually never barked – it's not considered genteel to bark coarsely, like a common dog.

I was very surprised when the police came; they turned out to be monsters! They actually took my master away! He was later convicted of the crime of murder. It was proven that he, and he alone, always put the olive in the glass for Felina. I could hardly believe my ears. I tried frantically to confess that it was I who had put the poisoned olive in the drink but, despite all my crying, my whining, my barking, my running round in frantic circles, the only result was a decision made that, as I was obviously mad, I should be put down.

Naturally, I was upset to know that I was going to the Great Kennel in the sky so early in my life, but on the actual day of the fatal injection I heard one officer tell another that my master, Bertram St Clare, was to be hanged that very same day for murder in the first degree. I was so happy at that news that I looked forward to the injection with impatience; we would be together again – this very day – for ever and ever.

And so we died, and so I should be able to say that we lived forever, happily ever after, but I had forgotten something. You most probably have guessed what it was.

Felina was there waiting for us! We three would be together for eternity!

My mind fled immediately to Shakespeare, and thus to Hamlet finding the skull of poor Yorick…

I began, 'Alas, poor Yorick…' No… Wait a minute! Wait a minute! No, that's not right – I can't continue with that. Damn, poor Yorick; he didn't have to face what I have to face…

I started again. 'Alas, poor Zuppy! I knew him, Horatio: a dog of infinite jest…

The Visiting Hour

'Bob! Look who's standing there!'

'Where, Dot?'

'Near Mum's bed, stupid. What the hell has Shirley done to her hair? It looks ridiculous. She's nearly fifty, not sixteen. Look at the colour. She's gone *blonde* again! It's so yellow she looks like a daffodil. With her wrinkles it ought to be grey.'

'Yes, I see them. But get a look at Harry! He's put on about twenty kilos, wouldn't you say'? He looks obese, the slob – they make a good pair, the both of them.'

'He always loved his food, the fat moron. I notice his eyebrows are still missing, so be careful what you say. Whatever Shirley saw in him, I'll never know, but Bob, take care with your words. You know why those two are here! They've never been before... Why Shirley, darling! How wonderful to see you, and looking so lovely, as usual. I'll just put these chocolates down here next to these beautiful flowers – they must be yours, aren't they? They're just...er...like you, so...so yellow. I do love yellow flowers. I'll just remove the price label. Oh, I do like your hair, Shirl. You look just as you did at high school. You make me jealous.'

'Dot, you don't think the blonde looks silly, do you? Harry put me off when I came home from the hair salon. He didn't like it, said it was too yellow but, if you do like it... You've always had good taste.'

'Oh, I *do* like it. We *both* do, don't we, Bob?'

'Yes, I was saying to Dot, as we stood in the doorway of the ward, "Who's that young woman with Harry near the bed?"'

'Really? Bob, that's so sweet of you. Did you hear that, Harry? Bob likes my hair.'

'He also likes tripe. Bob's never been a good judge of anything. You know what he advised me to do about those shares…'

'Aw, come on, Harry old pal. I had a good tip about those shares. You weren't the only one to lose on them. I lost a bundle myself…'

'That didn't comfort me much, Bob, while I was I applying for a new loan at the bank…'

'Oh, forget the silly shares, Harry. You know you promised me you wouldn't bring up those shares if we met Bob and Dot here at the hospital…'

'It's the principle of the thing. It was the same with the barbecue we bought. Bob insisted we buy the more expensive brand, and it's never worked properly…we spent all that money which I was saving to buy really classy wallpaper to re-do the hallway.'

'I'm sorry to correct you, Harry, you being my brother-in-law and everything, but my husband, Bob, was right there – I grant you, he's not right many times, but as regards the barbecue, he was spot on.'

'How can you say that, Dot? My Harry's very good with all those gadgets. Why, he fixed the kid next door's billycart in a flash, changed the wheel and everything. The course he did at the tech was wonderful. He scored very high marks. The instructor said he was so good, he should consider teaching the course.'

'It's a pity then, Shirley, that the course wasn't about learning to read the instructions on the barbecue before you turned on the gas…'

'Bob, what instructions? There were no instructions. I just had to make the thing start the best way I could…'

'What do you mean, Harry, there were no instructions? There was a little booklet just inside the lid. You could see if when you opened it.'

'Oh, that? I thought that was just to get the fire started. I put a match to it and turned the gas on… That's when I lost my eyebrows.'

'A perfectly natural mistake, Harry. Wasn't it, Bob? *Wasn't it?*

'Eh? Oh, yes, perfectly natural. Let's forget the barbecue. I most probably got it all wrong as usual. I think you look much better without the eyebrows – more macho. Tell me, how's the golf going?'

'Oh, yes, the golf. Well now, that's another thing altogether. I don't want to boast but last Thursday –'

'Now, Harry, sorry to interrupt, darling, but tell Bob and Dot what a wonderful thing you're doing! Oh, he's so shy. The big bear, I tell him he's become, with his new size, like a giant, cuddly bear.'

'Stop it, Shirley. You're embarrassing me.'

'Well, if you're not going to tell them, I will. Do you know what this great big baby I married is doing for his little wife?'

'No, do tell us, Shirley. We're dying to know. *Aren't* we, Bob?'

'Too right. I can hardly wait. Having difficulty breathing with the suspense. You may not be too good with barbecues, Harry, but you're a good bloke, and your heart's in the right place. Dot and I respect you –'

'Ooooooooooooooooh! Agh!'

'Goodness, Dot, what on earth was *that?*'

'It's Mum. Just be a little quieter, dear, there's a love. Shirley and I are having a nice little talk. I'm sorry, Shirl, you know what she's like.'

'Of course! Do I ever? Well, Dot, as I was trying to tell you before we were rudely interrupted, Harry, my dear, sweet, cuddly husband, is teaching me to play golf. There!'

'Really? Isn't that marvellous? I'm so envious, Shirl. The only thing Bob taught me was how to climb onto the roof to fix the aerial. I bet Harry's an absolute whiz as a teacher, too, Shirl. What do you say to that, Bob?'

'I would've said just what you did, Dot. Oh, Shirley, you are a lucky girl as well as looking beautiful!'

'Are you playing with a handicap, Shirley?'

'Well, Dot, the only handicap is Harry, actually… Hee, hee, Hee! I'm sorry. I simply couldn't resist the joke.'

'Don't apologise, Shirley. That's really funny, isn't it, Bob? *Isn't it?* Oh! What's the matter with you now?'

'I think it's your mother.'

'What do you mean, my mother? What about her?'

'Well, I'm sorry, Dot dearest, but I think she just died.'

'*What?* Shirley, isn't that just like her? Just when we were having a nice little chat. She always tries to spoil everything.'

'But what about the funeral, Dot? That's what I want to know. Who's going to pay for that? We'll have to go halves. Harry always said that cremation's the way to go.'

'Shirl, I think Harry's right: cremation is much cheaper, and quicker. What days are you free next week? Any days you're not doing anything?'

'Well, we have a golf day on Tuesday and I wouldn't want to miss that. I'd be free Monday. What about you?'

'Yes, I'm busy most of next week, but I could get off Monday, though, if we make it in the morning. Would that be all right? Bob has tickets for a movie Monday night. Let's make it Monday. But what are you doing, Bob?'

'These chocolates, Dot. There's no point in leaving them now, is there? I'll just pop them in my pocket. Harry, what about your flowers?'

'Shirley, take the flowers back home. They could easily be revived with an aspirin in the water. They'll do for Monday. It's silly to waste money Look out, Dot, here comes the boss!'

'Yes, Sister, I understand. It happened just as we were praying around her bed, the poor old soul. However, I'm sure she was comforted by seeing her children with her at the end. Well, my sister, Shirley and her husband, Harry, have been marvellous…but yes, you're right, it is a shock even though we were expecting it at any moment, but then…you know how it is. Thank you. We're very grateful to everyone here. Everyone has been wonderful, and so understanding.'

'Is she gone? Oh, good! Well, I'm sorry, Shirley and Harry. It's been lovely talking to you both but I'm so upset. I think I'll have to go. Bob and I will just have a quiet drink somewhere on our own – possibly in the meditation gardens near the train station urinal – on our way home. I'm sorry to sniffle, but it is a shock, isn't it? Bye. Bye.

*

'Are they still watching, Bob? No? Good! Let's get out of this joint. I've got to pick up a hot chicken on the way home for tea. Or do you feel like Indian for a change?'